"I'm so frightene[d]
I want my life back."

Locke knelt next to Greer. "I'm scared, too, if it makes you feel any better. For Lin's safety and yours. But he's been in this house. He knows we have a daughter, and while we're being super careful and taking extra measures to make sure we aren't followed...we aren't perfect."

She looked into his eyes and he saw her fear.

"Maybe we move Lin somewhere else," he told her. "Or talk to the sheriff about extra protection. We'll figure it out. You and me," he whispered. "Okay?"

She only nodded and he refrained from wiping her tearstained cheeks. He was supposed to be angry with her for keeping his child from him. But right now, in this moment, she was so vulnerable. So frightened. He could only offer her compassion. Any other emotion he felt toward Greer could get them killed.

He had to focus on one thing only: a killer was coming. With vengeance on his mind.

Jessica R. Patch lives in the Mid-South, where she pens inspirational contemporary romance and romantic suspense novels. When she's not hunched over her laptop or going on adventurous trips with willing friends in the name of research, you can find her watching way too much Netflix with her family and collecting recipes for amazing dishes she'll probably never cook. To learn more about Jessica, please visit her at jessicarpatch.com.

Books by Jessica R. Patch

Love Inspired Suspense

Fatal Reunion
Protective Duty
Concealed Identity
Final Verdict
Cold Case Christmas
Killer Exposure

The Security Specialists

Deep Waters
Secret Service Setup
Dangerous Obsession

Visit the Author Profile page at Harlequin.com.

KILLER EXPOSURE

JESSICA R. PATCH

HARLEQUIN® LOVE INSPIRED® SUSPENSE

Recycling programs
for this product may
not exist in your area.

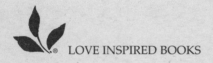

LOVE INSPIRED BOOKS

ISBN-13: 978-1-335-67897-3

Killer Exposure

www.Harlequin.com

Printed in U.S.A.

Be strong and of a good courage, fear not, nor be afraid of them: for the Lord thy God, he it is that doth go with thee; he will not fail thee, nor forsake thee.
–Deuteronomy 31:6

To Mom, for loving us kids sacrificially and unconditionally, and letting me sit out on the porch as a kid watching thunderstorms instead of making me come in the house.

Special thanks to my agent, Rachel Kent, who's always in my corner and a joy to work with. To Shana Asaro, for her excitement about weather disaster plots and for always being a rock star editor; to Emily Rodmell, for her help early on in the story; to Susan Tuttle—the other half of my author brain and human shovel always ready to dig me out of a plot hole; and to Jill Kemerer, for helping me burrow into my heroine's and hero's hearts to find their fears.

ONE

Spring wasn't the only thing in the air. Storms were rolling in, and if Greer Montgomery didn't need the money she wouldn't be standing here in the middle of a field on an April evening taking photos for the upgraded Goldenville Chamber of Commerce website. Nope, she'd be home snuggled up with her own little Stormie Lin, listening to her suck a pacifier and inhaling that sweet baby scent—a mix of innocence and baby powder. But Greer would work three more jobs, if necessary, to provide for her nine-month-old princess.

The Stellar Entertainment traveling carnival had spent most of last night and early this morning setting up for the week-long spring-fest. Greer had been by earlier to catch some of the action and meet with the Chamber of Commerce's executive director—and her friend—Cindy Woolridge to discuss the vision for the website.

Most of the patrons tonight would be donning

ponchos and rain boots. Alabama's springs could be wet and soggy. But that didn't stop families from coming out in droves to indulge in corn dogs—or, as everyone around here called them, Pronto Pups—pretzels, rigged games, a Ferris wheel and cotton candy. Greer peered into the sky. The sun had been eclipsed by thunderheads that looked a lot like spun cotton candy piled high on a stick. Breaking through the dappled clouds, lightning flashed in the distance. The scent of rain rolled in, which brought a whole different flood of emotions.

She clicked a few photos of the lit-up Ferris wheel. Perfect for the chamber website. Tourists would want to come and visit; folks moving to the area would see how family-friendly Goldenville was. Southern hospitality at its best. When she returned home a year and a half ago, she'd been welcomed with open arms. One set of feeble arms had belonged to her mother. Greer had expected to come home temporarily to help her after a mild heart attack, but Mama never completely recovered and three months ago, she'd passed into the strong arms of Jesus after a severe heart attack. Greer missed her daily. Missed that Lin wouldn't get a chance to know her grandmother.

Another flash of lightning, accompanied by a peal of thunder, revealed the storm was fast approaching. Maybe less than thirty minutes. Greer had already taken a ton of photos this morning after her shift at the sheriff's department. She normally worked days, but they were short a few deputies, so she'd taken the overtime and worked the night shift last night. Not much in town too sinister. Other than those thunderheads.

Locke would call them by their proper name— cumulonimbus clouds. Her tummy flip-flopped at the thought of him. But she'd been thinking about him all afternoon. She'd have never experienced a storm in all its terrifying glory if she hadn't chased dozens with him over the few years they were together. Seen them through his shockingly blue eyes—blue like tropical waters with limbuses as black as a tempest.

She wandered through the maze of rides, games and food stands. Carnies worked to get set up. Music blared through speakers, and she gravitated toward employee campers and then to the field that widened into the woods—which gave her some unique photo opportunities to capture storms, clouds or any wild weather through the treetops. Locke taught her that, too. But their dreams of exploring the world and capturing it on film had shattered like glass in a hailstorm.

She had planned to come home and nurse Mama back to health while Locke went on with the research team, documenting storm systems and tornadoes. Then she would meet back up with him and the team, helping with photography needs.

But upon arriving back in Goldenville, she discovered a shared moment of weakness with Locke—that she sorely regretted—had left her pregnant. But God had been faithful to forgive and to provide for her and Lin, whom she did not regret one iota. Lin was the good in the whole messy situation.

Greer had quickly secured a job as a crime-scene photographer and sheriff's deputy. Law enforcement was in the blood. From her mama's side of the family—the Buchanan side. Dad hadn't been one for enforcing anything. That was Mama's job. Then he'd flown the coop decades ago, only coming back to town to visit her and her older brother, Hollister, on occasion. But eventually he became as scarce as woodland creatures before a cyclone.

She snapped a few photos of the lightning to use with her new filters. Thunder rumbled as she darted in between the employees' makeshift homes. A commotion came from one of the smaller house trailers up ahead. Not much light due to the sun setting and the blanket of ominous clouds. Greer crept toward the sounds of a scuffle.

The door was cracked open.

A man's garbled cry sent chill bumps across Greer's skin. She drew her off-duty Glock 43 and darted toward the camper, swinging open the door.

A man stared at her, his eyes inky and threatening. Her training kicked in. "Drop the knife. Hands up. Come out slowly. *Slowly*," she commanded.

Dressed in a carnival maintenance uniform, he held up black-gloved hands, one still gripping the bloody blade. He wore a ball cap that hid his hair, but his short-cropped beard and mustache matched his eyes, his physical features distorted in the dimness.

The man at his feet stared blankly, unmoving. The amount of blood couldn't have come from only one wound. He'd been stabbed multiple times. Greer feared she'd witnessed his last breath, last sound. "Take it easy. You're under arrest." No radio to call it in. But she had the situation under control. Once she got him to lie face down with his hands behind his back, she'd use her cell and get backup out here to cuff him.

A brilliant flash of lightning popped across the sky. The man kicked a bucket through the door. She batted it away, but it startled her. The killer leaped out and ran for the woods. Greer couldn't let him get away. She rushed inside the mobile home and checked the victim's vitals. As she sadly suspected—gone.

Sprinting through the light drops of rain, Greer spied him rushing into the safety of the trees.

"Freeze!" She raced in his direction. Eating up the field, she flew into the dense forest and paused, listening. A whiz up ahead. She moved in.

He disappeared.

Her heart pounded as she crept through the trees, brush, limbs and leaves crunching under her feet.

Come on. I need another flash of lightning. Come. On.

A burst of light shot through the night, and the man slammed her into a tree. Greer's loose grip, due to the rain, was lost, and her gun plummeted into the brush. She swung at the killer and connected with his jaw with a right uppercut. She might be slight in frame, but her brother had been a Navy SEAL, and he'd taught her a trick or two—and she'd been kickboxing since her early twenties.

A raspy laugh belched from his mouth, and the knife he'd refused to drop glinted in the night. Her adrenaline kicked up a notch. Game changer.

She weaved and dodged him, hoping to spot

her gun with a fresh flick of light. The camera hanging around her neck thumped against her chest.

No go. Jumping backward, she grabbed a large, gnarly branch and swung it at the attacker. Thoughts of her baby girl recharged her need to fight. The killer rushed her, and she tripped in the darkness, dropping the limb. They tumbled to the ground, and she screeched. But no one would hear. Not this far out. Not over the thunder. Not over the carnival music blaring.

Greer had no one to rely on to survive but herself and God. She screamed again as he shoved her into the dead winter twigs and pinecones. They cut into the back of her cropped denim jacket and T-shirt with a sharp sting. She drew up her knees, putting one against his stomach, blocking him from putting his whole body and weight on top of her. He grabbed her right wrist. She snatched his with her left hand, pulling his arm across her body and pushing with her free leg. She rolled out from under him, her camera strap snapping and sending it to the forest floor. Scrambling to her feet, she sprang into action and tore through the trees as the raindrops turned into a steady, but drizzly, rain.

Breathing ragged. Fear propelling her forward, faster. Stronger. Greer's lungs screamed for more air, burning in protest. She'd left her hair down, and it matted to her face and eyes.

She glanced back as lightning illuminated the surroundings. He was ten feet away, closing in. Zigzagging, she smacked straight into a tree and bounced off, falling to the ground and landing with a heavy thud.

"Whoa." The tree spoke. "Hey!" This time the voice roared, and she raised her head to see the man-tree go after the killer. Pushing hair from her eyes, Greer heaved breaths and struggled to get up. He dove onto the guy, and the attacker rolled him over. But he was quick and easy on his feet. He jumped up and put himself in a defensive position to block. Martial arts? The guy swung, but her rescuer blocked him once, twice, then landed a frontal kick, propelling him backward. There was some definite power in those legs.

"Who do you think you are?" he hollered, disgust and something familiar in his tone.

Greer's head pounded, and her entire body blazed and ached.

The killer rushed him, and as fast as the lightning was striking, the towering oak used a series of hand motions to nail him on the ground. "Stay down!"

No. Greer stood, tottered. Couldn't be. Had to

be the blows to the head… But that voice. That confident, almost arrogant attitude. "Locklin?"

He whipped his head in her direction. "*Greer…?* Greer!"

The attacker made his move, and before Greer could warn Locke, he swept Locke's feet out from under him, throwing him off balance, then bolted and fled through the woods.

Locke raced toward her as she teetered, legs like noodles. Nauseated. Headache. Trembling. He righted her as the sky lit up.

His crow-colored hair was a bit longer, shaggier, framing his face and touching his collar. Cheeks, chin and neck were scruffier. But it was storm-chasing season. A camera hung around his neck. "How bad are you hurt?" His hands roamed her face, head, back, arms.

She shrugged him away. His touch, while medically motivated, felt too intimate. Too familiar. Too perfect and safe. "I'm fine."

"You're shaking…and bleeding." He brushed her hair from her face.

"Stop touching me." She jerked back.

"Okay, I'm backing off." He held his hands up as a boom of thunder breached the wooded barrier.

"Sorry. I didn't mean to bite your head off. I'm just…rattled. But fine." That wasn't completely true. Greer was far from fine. Things were happening so fast. She'd been attacked. Locke Gallagher was here. The past was rushing in, as were thoughts of what she needed to do now as a law enforcer. She was flustered, panicked and afraid.

"I get it, Greer. We gotta go, though. Now."

She nodded, snagged her cell phone from her denim-jacket pocket and turned on her flashlight. "I need my gun and camera. Help me find them?" She hurried and called in the crime, giving the last known location of the killer and which camper the victim would be in.

Locke stood like a statue, rain slicking his hair to his face.

"Please," she begged. "I have to get back to the crime scene. Get photos."

Locke shoved rain-drenched hair from his face. "What is going on?" His words were laced with frustration.

"Did you not hear me call it in? I witnessed him murdering an employee. With this weather, time isn't on my side." She searched the area for her gun and camera, rain soaking her to the bone.

Locke finally helped her. "Here." He found the gun by the tree.

"Thank you." She needed to answer his questions. Have some kind of conversation. He'd have a million questions, but rain would wash away possible evidence, and a killer was on the loose. She had to focus on her job first, then she'd muster some courage to talk to Locke. "What are you even doing here, in town? In these woods?" she asked as she found her camera, then jogged through the woods and into the field to the campers.

He kept her pace.

Locke couldn't be here. Not in Goldenville. Not now. Not ever.

"I'm chasing a cluster of storms in the surrounding areas. Be about a week or so."

That was too long. This was a small town. He'd no doubt bump into Greer at the store, a café, the park. And he'd see Lin.

And he'd know he had daughter. A daughter he'd never laid eyes on. Never met.

Because Greer had kept it a secret.

To spare their child from the future heartache of knowing she was never wanted by her father.

Locke ran with Greer across the field to the carnival employee campground. Rows upon rows of RVs and campers created a temporary home base for the traveling crew. Locke was no stranger to this kind of living. Especially during spring and summer storm seasons. Greer was supposed to be on the team, too. But she'd come home to help her mother and dropped him faster than a twister descending out of the sky, ignoring all his calls and texts. He'd taken the obvious hint that things were over, which shattered his heart in a million pieces. He'd been too cowardly to show up on her doorstep and face the rejection in person. It had been easier to lick his wounds alone and fake it until he made it.

He'd been debating giving her a courtesy voicemail, as she wouldn't answer his calls, to let her know that he'd be in her hometown for a week or so with the group of scientists he worked with. Could he slip into town for the week and her not know it? He was leaning toward "yes," when Greer had literally smacked into him in the woods. No hiding now.

Locke had been capturing this small storm on his own time. The earlier weather hadn't been conducive to tornadoes so he'd been using it in his free time to collect photos for his online web gallery. He'd created a large platform and made a name for himself as a storm photographer. Even *National Geographic* had purchased a few images and done a piece on him and his role working with this team to discover more about why some storms produce tornadoes and others don't. They were working to help stretch tornado warning times for people.

He hadn't expected to find Greer. Certainly not battling a crazed dude in the woods. He thought he'd heard screams earlier and was making his way toward them when Greer had slammed into him. Then he'd seen the attacker and realized the woman was in serious danger. He hadn't known it was Greer until she'd called him by his full first name. Locklin. He'd been so stunned and distracted that the man got away. How had she witnessed the crime? Why was she hanging out around employee living grounds and why was she calling in crimes like it was her...?

"Do you work for the police now?"

They dashed through a row of campers, and Greer slowed down. "Sheriff's department. Deputy and crime-scene photographer when they need one. Thus, me needing to get photos."

Locke had met her in one of their criminal justice classes, but they'd gotten to know each other working for the college paper. "Isn't that a conflict of interest since you're a witness to this crime?"

"Are you serious right now? It's about to storm. I'm the only one around. Who else is going to do it?"

She had a point. And it wasn't like Locke was in law enforcement now. He'd dropped out. School wasn't for him, and he never wanted to follow the Gallagher-Flynn lineage into the military and law enforcement. Locke just chased storms and had disappointed everyone, as usual, including Dad. God rest his soul.

Greer shined a light and entered the gloomy scene. Locke followed but stayed outside the door. He wasn't dumb enough to contaminate a crime scene. The deceased was lying in a pool of blood. This right here—this was why Locke never wanted to go into the criminal justice field. His stomach wasn't fragile, but he detested violence. The marring of humans. The evil. His heart couldn't handle this day in and day out.

Dad would probably consider it weak. Locke simply didn't like looking at death every single day. Greer used a broom handle to lift debris and then she went to work clicking the camera as if she hadn't been chased and attacked in the woods. He admired her tenacity. Her drive to help fight injustice.

But Locke would rather use his camera to capture the terrifying glory of a whirlwind. Even in the wake of its destruction, there was still beauty and wonder to be found. In that tragedy, communities rallied to support one another. He had hundreds of photos of humanity doing its best.

Police sirens sounded.

"Who was this guy?" Locke asked, and studied Greer. Maybe she wasn't as held together—he caught her hands trembling.

"Don't know yet."

"You probably need a doctor or something."

She paused and poked her head outside the camper; a gentleness softened her features. "I sincerely appreciate your concern. But honestly, Locklin, I'm good. I'm not trying to ignore you. I just… I gotta work. Gotta do the job and it helps me not think about the fact I almost bit it out there tonight."

The thought of that sent a shock to his system. But if she said she was okay, he'd go with it. Greer was a strong woman. She wasn't blowing him off like she had almost two years ago. He'd try to be more patient. Patience wasn't exactly a virtue he possessed, though. It required being still and Locke had always struggled with being still. School, church, events and the list went on. He was full of energy and always antsy. Just the way he was made.

Lights flashed in the distance. Sheriff's deputies had arrived. They went to work sealing off the scene and forcing Locke to the other side of the tape, where he stood in the rain getting wetter with each second. A chill had already numbed his skin but he wasn't going anywhere. Not until he was sure she was safe. Didn't matter that other police were around and were capable.

"Sir," another crime tech said. "I need to collect evidence from your hands. Deputy Montgomery said you hit the attacker's face. I'd like to

get a sample before this storm washes it away."
Locke complied while the officer did his thing.
Another deputy walked up—he was an inch
shorter than Locke's six-foot-one frame. "I'm
Deputy Crisp."

"Locke Gallagher."

"I'm gonna need your statement. I've already
gotten Deputy Montgomery's."

Locke gave him the lowdown, while keeping
an eye on Greer as she talked with other deputies.

When Greer finally slipped out from under
the tape, he headed straight for her.

She cocked her head. "You don't have to stick
around, Locke. They got everything they needed
and as I said before, I'm okay." She sighed and
reached into her pocket, pulling out a small
pouch. She tossed it to him. "Poncho. Though,
it's a little late for staying dry." A smirk pulled
at her lips as if she was totally fine, but her eyes
betrayed her.

"I know I don't need to stay. I want to. And
I know you too well. You're not okay." It was
clear Greer didn't want anything to do with him.
He got that. He'd repeatedly been over her reasons for going cold turkey on him. She might
have changed her mind about the traveling life.
And the bigger one—the night they'd crossed a
line—could have seriously factored into her not

returning. He'd made a huge mistake. Shouldn't have let it get so out of control. Epic fail on his part and he blamed himself completely. Not that he hadn't moved on since she'd broken his heart—he had—but of all the adventures Locke ever loved, Greer was his greatest. Couldn't they even be friends?

"Greer, I should have known you'd be here working." A tall man with thick silver hair approached. Locke hung back but could still hear the conversation.

"Hey, Sheriff. I'm not letting this one get away." She told him what happened. "What we know right now is the vic's name is Fred 'Flip' Bomer. He's worked the Stellar Entertainment carnival for eight years. Done an array of things from games to running the bumper cars. Thirty-seven. Not married. The carnival manager, Rudy Dennison, is getting us his file, but you know that's going to be thin. Carnivals don't require background checks or too much information."

"True. Listen, I appreciate you taking the initiative and getting the photos, but you were attacked. Get some rest. Let Crisp take it from here." The fatherly figure laid a hand on her shoulder. "You sure you don't need medical attention?"

Greer bristled. "No, sir. I'm going to work with Burt on a sketch of the man who killed

Flip and attacked me. Manager said they have multiple maintenance workers on staff. We're rounding them up now. I need to stay on this. Need to ID this guy."

He seemed to debate the idea. "Let Crisp and Garrison do it. When they get the workers corralled, you can make the ID." He gave her a slight side-hug. "Glad you're okay." He then turned to Locke. "Sheriff Randy Wright."

"Locke Gallagher."

"Thank you for being in the woods." He squinted, rain dripping off his poncho. "Why *were* you out here in the woods?"

Locke glanced at Greer. The truth was he was trying to figure out what to do about seeing or not seeing her while photographing nature. "I'm with a group researching storms. Y'all have several supercells coming in this week, prime weather for twisters. I photograph them."

"A storm chaser?"

"Yes, sir."

He grinned. "Glad you were here. Not that I don't think Greer could have made it out, but sometimes we need a little help."

"I guess so."

The sheriff shook his hand again and left them alone as the rain let up. Wasn't over yet, though. "Locke, I'm safe. Seriously, you can get back to what you were doing," Greer said.

"I know." But he didn't want to leave. "How long will the sketch take? I can wait. We can get dry…and get coffee?"

"I'm not sure. And I worked all last night, picking up overtime, so I'm pretty tired." As if on cue, she yawned, then sheepishly grinned. His heart slammed into his throat. Those wide, thick lips on a heart-shaped face. The straightest nose he'd ever seen. Her chocolate-brown eyes revealed true exhaustion. But there wasn't a measure of fear in her tone—she was so like the Greer he used to know. Used to love.

Overtime and exhaustion, he understood. "Okay…well, maybe sometime this week?"

She shifted and shoved a thick mass of wet hair from her face. It still cascaded past her shoulders all in one length. Probably the same corn-silk blond, but now damp from rain it was the color of sand after the ocean washed over it. Man, he'd loved her hair. "I'm going to be pretty tied up now with this case."

"Too tied up you can't eat?"

"I work more than one job, Locke. I'm a part-time photographer. Family portraits, senior pictures, community events. You know, the kind you never wanted to be. The kind that boxed you into nine-to-five."

He had said that. There was too much adventure in life to settle down and do one single thing every day. Too many places to see, too much to experience. Not a single storm was the same. The thrill. The challenge. Locke did what he wanted, when he wanted. At one time, Greer was onboard and living that life with him. And they were having fun, were happy. "There's no challenge in that," he teased.

"Try getting four children under the age of six to all sit still and face the camera and smile at the same time." She half laughed, but it seemed sad. "It's not the wild adventure you chase, but it's satisfying. I like documenting family milestones and memories. I like keeping my town and county safe. I like the people. I like this life."

Whole lotta like. No mention of love. Once, she'd told Locke she loved chasing storms. Loved capturing them. Loved…him. "I'm glad you're happy, Greer. I've never wanted anything else. I guess…guess it just stinks you couldn't be happy with me." There, he said it. "But I'm over it." She needed to know he wasn't going to be stalking her and groveling. She'd made clear what she wanted. And he wasn't a part of it. "If that's what's holdin' you back from having a meal or coffee with me. Friends is cool. I can do friends."

Greer cleared her throat, glanced away. "Good, okay," she whispered. "I'll… I'll think about it."

Better than "get lost." "Hey, you witnessed

a murder tonight. This guy…are you worried he'll come back?" She was clearly worried about something. Would he try to finish her off? The thought sent a blip of panic to his chest. "You want me to see you home?"

"No." A flash of fear splashed through her eyes. "I appreciate the offer, but I can see myself home."

"Not saying you aren't capable or anything." He shrugged.

"We'll find this guy, Locke. Probably tonight. I'm not worried." She lowered the hood of her poncho now that the rain had stopped. She wasn't fooling Locke. Greer's hand had a tremor and the truth showed in her eyes. She wasn't only shaken, she was scared. It *had* crossed her mind that he would try and finish the job. Even if it was a fleeting thought. It was there. Locke could read it on her face. "I have to get back to work."

An awkward silence ballooned around them.

"Be careful chasing those storms," she said. "Hope you find what you're looking for, but also I kind of hope you don't." She grinned. Genuine again. Sincere.

No one wanted tornadoes ravaging their towns, and about twelve years ago, three had come through this county, tearing them to pieces. A state of emergency had been declared.

But over time, the community had rebuilt, with some outside help. That's why this research was so important.

"And thank you. For...being in the woods and coming to my aid. All that martial arts training paid off."

Finally, a real thank-you. The soft side of Greer. The side he'd always admired. One of the many facets he fell in love with. "Well, when you have uncontainable, boundless energy and your dad's military, and a cop, he finds a way to burn it off and prepare you for your calling." One he never felt called to. He ran his hand through his wet hair and shivered. "But you're welcome."

"I really gotta go now."

With that, she spun and disappeared into the rain-soaked night.

Sitting in her car, soggy, freezing, exhausted and sore, Greer laid her head on the driver's seat and closed her eyes. After stomping away from Locke, she'd worked with the sketch artist and hung around a little longer at the scene until Sheriff Wright basically tossed her in the car and sent her home. Too much had happened tonight. Death. Her near-death and then Locke showing up. She was grateful that he'd been there. His usual self. Brave. Kind. A little snarky and humorous and attentive. For being a man she was sure had ADHD, he never seemed to have an issue giving her his undivided attention, and it hurt beyond belief, so she'd avoided him. Old feelings. Fear. Guilt. Locke had a daughter, and he didn't even know. He'd never wanted children. He'd been adamant about that up front. They got in the way and wouldn't fit into his lifestyle—his words. They would cramp everything. So Greer had taken the chicken's way out and not told him.

But tonight proved in a small way that she had made the right decision to protect her daughter by not telling him the truth. He'd said it himself, years ago—he would not be boxed in. Locke had always rebelled against social norms and family expectations. He wanted to live the way he chose. No chains. No being tied to what the world said being an adult ought to look like. And no children.

They'd been dating a year when the conversation came up again about having a family, and it had turned into an argument. Locke hadn't changed his mind and never would. Greer had been so head over heels in love with him that she'd agreed and wouldn't bring it up again. But Greer had always wanted a family. A husband who wouldn't leave. Who wanted his child always and forever. Clearly, that man wasn't Locke. She'd considered breaking it off after that last heated discussion, but she'd loved him too much and couldn't make the tough choice.

Then Mama got sick. And she found out she was pregnant. That made the decision for her.

Besides, Locke was finally getting his dream, making a mark on the storm-photography world. Greer didn't want to rob him of that. But mostly, she was terrified he would give it all up for them and one day he'd do exactly what her father had done—abandon them. Locke would feel imprisoned by his own daughter. Greer's pregnancy would be nothing but a trap, a means to get her way of having a family—at least that's how he'd eventually see it. He'd blame his child and Greer for all the years he lost. Just like Dad. Then he would walk out and Lin would have to live with the same fear, the same guilt, the same heartache as Greer. Dad's words to Mama echoed in Greer's ears every day.

"You got pregnant and trapped me! I never wanted this life. I want to do what I want. I want my life back." And Dad had left Mama.

And Greer and her older brother, Hollister.

The pain had been overwhelming. Greer would never let Lin experience that kind of heartache. She was no one's prison. She would never have to grow up feeling unwanted or unloved. Greer would never reject and abandon her.

But now, as she sat in her driveway, she wondered how in the world she was going to keep Locke from finding out. Deep in the marrow of her bones, a whisper formed that he had every right to know and always had.

Fear held her hostage from listening to it.

She climbed from her vehicle, exhausted. Her best friend, Tori, had already offered to keep Lin for the night since it was so late, and she was available to watch her tomorrow. Tori's job as a nurse at the hospital allowed her to keep Lin a couple of days and nights a week, depending on what shift she was working. Greer didn't have a lot of money for day care, so she appreciated having friends who could help. She still had medical bills for Mama. A house payment. Insurance. Ugh. The thought of bills only further soured her mood.

Trudging up the walkway to the small home Mama had lived in, Greer held back tears. Being a single mama was no joke. No one to help her. No one to help carry the pressures of daily life, finances or parenting. Fear and dread of how she was going to manage each day, how she was going to provide for Lin. But she wouldn't change it. And she'd move heaven and earth to make sure Lin was happy and had everything she needed to feel loved and successful. Like her own mama had, working extra shifts and jobs at Christmas to provide for Greer and Hollister.

As children they'd never appreciated or understood the sacrifices Mama had made.

Greer knew now.

She unlocked the front door and entered. Still
smelled like Mama's White Diamonds perfume.
The ache swept through her empty stomach and
clutched her ribs.

As she switched on the lamp in the cozy living room, Greer's hairs on her arms rose. She
froze and scanned the area. Nothing looked out
of place. Her adrenaline raced again. Too much
commotion and devastation tonight. She was
paranoid.

Creeping down the small hallway, she entered the only bathroom in the two-bedroom
home and switched on the shower to scalding
hot, then closed the door to let the steam rise.
Greer popped into the nursery, turned on the
light and inhaled Lin's scent. She missed her
baby girl. She entered her bedroom, which the
bathroom separated from Lin's, and stripped off
her outer hoodie, tossing it into the hall to wash.
Tomorrow was going to be a long day. She had
dozens of carnies to question. Hopefully they'd
find this guy tonight. Maybe she should have
stuck around regardless. But she was no good
to anyone or to the investigation right now with
so little sleep.

Hairs on her neck spiked.

She whirled toward the closet, reaching for her gun as the killer from the woods lunged and knocked her to the bedroom floor before she could grab it.

TWO

Locke haphazardly punched his steering wheel, sighed and raked a hand through his hair. He needed a haircut, but during storm-chasing season he didn't pay attention to haircuts or daily shaving. He was parked down the street from Greer's. It wasn't hard to find. Not when he'd been here before.

It was after midnight, and the last thing Locke wanted to do was wake up Greer's mom, especially since she was in bad health. But after going back to the camper park, showering and getting dry clothes on, he couldn't concentrate on a single thing. He had this ball in his gut that kept signaling red flags.

Locke groaned and went with his gut. He turned his lights off as he pulled behind Greer's silver CR-V. If she still had the same bedroom, he could tap on her window. Probably terrify her after what happened earlier tonight, but he didn't want to wake the entire house. He slipped around back and tiptoed to the room Greer had slept in when he visited.

Greer screamed.

Locke's heart leaped into his throat.

Another shrill scream, but it came from outside. Hurrying, he rushed around the side of the house as Greer bolted through the patio doors.

The killer burst through after her, clobbering her to the ground.

Blood turning hot and adrenaline spiking, Locke flew to the attacker and grabbed him by the collar, then hurled him into the air and two feet from Greer. He landed with a thud and a curse. Stalking toward him, Locke had no intentions of letting this creep get away again.

The guy hopped to his feet and raced behind the house toward the neighbor's. Locke gave chase. With every stride, he grew angrier. How dare this guy try to come back? No one was going to hurt Greer. No one.

Locke gained on him as he hurdled a chain link fence into a backyard. Locke scaled the fence and turned the corner. Something smacked him upside the head, knocking him to the ground in a daze. He glanced down. The aluminum lid to a trash can was lying beside him. A flash of the attacker sprang over another fence.

Giving his head a good shake, Locke stood and rubbed his cheek. That was going to bring a nice, fat headache in a few hours. Greer might be hurt, and the attacker was now too far away to chase. Locke ran back to her house. This time, he knocked on the side patio door that she'd run through.

Greer opened it, looking worse for wear, hair hanging in knotted clumps. Same wet clothing she'd had on earlier. Dirt, grime and tears streaked her face. Her hands shook uncontrollably. Without thinking, he yanked her to him and crushed her in an embrace. She winced, and he eased up. "Greer," he whispered. "Are you hurt? Did he… Did he hurt you?"

She sniffed against his chest. She'd always fit perfectly, her head coming right under his chin. "No. I haven't been home long enough to go through this again."

"How did he get in?" Locke asked.

"Everything looked fine when I got home, but the window to the laundry room was broken. He got in through there."

How would the attacker know where she lived if he was a maintenance worker at the carnival?

"I don't suppose it would be too difficult to find out where I live. It's a small town. He couldn't have followed me. He was here when I got home."

Guess she'd been thinking the same thing. The

sound of the shower running caught his attention. "Did you call it in?"

"Yes. Deputy Crisp is out searching for him. I'm assuming he got away." She didn't pull away from him, and the familiarity pooled like warm goodness in his stomach.

"He did. Which reminds me. Can I have a couple pain relievers?"

Greer broke the hug and peered up at him. Lightly, she touched his cheek with her quaking fingers. She caught his eye, and their gazes held. Suddenly, she wrenched her hand away and strode to the cabinet by the fridge. "What did he get you with?" She fetched him two ibuprofens and a bottle of water.

"Metal trash lid."

"Ouch." She grabbed a pack of frozen peas from the freezer and handed them to him. "You'll want this."

Locke scanned the kitchen. The house was quiet. Too quiet. "Where's your mama? Is she okay?"

Greer looked away. "She—she passed three months ago. Another heart attack."

His stomach bottomed out. "Greer. I'm… I'm so sorry." She hadn't called him, which smarted, but not as much as it hurt to see her breaking. Greer and her mama had been close. The whole family had been after their dad left. He didn't know the entire story. Greer never spoke of him, but it had been a devastating blow to them all. "I know what you're going through." His dad had been gone much longer, but the emptiness was always there. He wished Greer would have called. Leaned on him. He could have helped her.

She wiped her eyes.

He placed his bottle of water on the sink. A wall of awkwardness built between them. "Why don't you go get dry and warm, and I'll make us some coffee or something. Then I'll fix that window."

Greer glanced behind her and a new wave of fear covered her face.

"Hey, don't worry. I won't let him hurt you, and I doubt he'll be back." Tonight. But he had a sneaky feeling this wasn't over. This guy was set on taking out the one witness to a murder, and he didn't seem to care that Greer worked for the sheriff's department. That made him brazen. Bold. Locke wasn't going anywhere.

"It's not that," she whispered. "I'll be right back and—and we should talk, Locklin. A major conversation."

Locke swallowed down a mountain of nerves. Well, he'd wanted answers. Guess he was about to get them. "I'll make it strong then."

"You definitely should." Worry etched her

brow. "And you don't have to stay. You…won't want to." She muttered the last part and he wasn't sure he heard right. Nothing could make him leave.

"Greer, a man tried to kill you multiple times tonight. Let's just say what we both know. He has no intention of letting you walk away after having seen him." He wasn't trying to scare her, but she was acting delusional. "Your colleagues obviously didn't solve the case after you left. I'm not leaving you alone. I want to stay."

"I'm trained."

"I don't care." He wasn't budging.

"The department is going to do drive-bys every thirty minutes. Fingerprint the window. I'm not scared."

Liar. She was terrified. He just wasn't sure why some of that fear seemed to be directed toward him. "Go take care of yourself. The only way you're getting rid of me is to call the police and say I'm trespassing, and after I saved you twice tonight, that feels like a crummy and ungrateful thing to do," he jested, trying to lighten her up, to relieve some fear and tension. He would keep her safe. "I may not be a gun-toting cop or Navy SEAL, but I'm more than capable of holding my own and watching out for you."

Greer inhaled deeply. "I know. Now, you make coffee and I'll only be a second."

"Okay," he offered and slowly moved to the fridge, taking out a carton of eggs. "I'll be right here making *eggs* and coffee." And trying to figure out what on earth was going on.

She rushed from the kitchen.

Locke laid the carton of eggs on the counter, then peeped into the living room and down the hall. The door to a bedroom closed. Back in the living room, a baby swing and toys littered the floor. She'd said she had side jobs. Was she babysitting or running a day care? The wall above the couch caught his eye.

A collage of photos. Those weren't there the last time he visited. There had been a huge painting of a meadow. He remembered because he'd loved it. It was only missing a tornado right down the middle.

He switched on the lamp by the couch and gaped.

Blood whooshed in his ears, leaving him dizzy. Photo after photo of a baby girl. Newborn pictures. One in a little tin washtub chewing on a rubber duck. But it wasn't the clever poses that nearly brought him to his knees. It was the black-as-night hair. The blue eyes that stared back at him. The dimple in her right cheek. Locke touched his right cheek, felt the dimple there.

His sight landed on a newborn picture with footprints and handprints beside it and a birthdate.

No. Didn't take a professor to do the math.

This child was nine months old.

Nine months of pregnancy.

Eighteen months ago, Greer had left him.

Why? Why would she do this? He lifted the most recent photo from the wall. Even without a DNA test, it was crystal clear that this child belonged to Locke.

He was a father.

He had a daughter.

His eyes burned and moisture blurred the photo in front of him. He blinked and focus came back. He trailed his index finger over the baby's face. She was… She was the most beautiful thing he'd ever seen. Mischief in her eyes already. She had Greer's thick lips and straight little nose.

His lungs squeezed. Emotions swept through him like a roller coaster. Pride. Joy. Fear. Confusion. Despair. Loss.

Anger.

He camped on anger. How could Greer do this? Keep him from his child. From being a dad. Was she never going to tell him? What if he'd never shown up in her hometown? What if he'd come by tonight and she hadn't been attacked? Would Greer have even let him inside?

"I was hoping to tell you before you saw all this," she whispered.

He pivoted and held up the photo.

Greer slid her gaze from the photo to Locke's face and her lip trembled, but she didn't speak. Didn't try to explain or toss a weak excuse his way.

"Where is she?" Fear flooded him. "Is she here?" Was she in the house when a killer broke in? His heart galloped, and he stormed down the hall, taking a hard left and flipping on the light in the room Greer had once used.

A perfect pink-and-pastel nursery came into view. He smelled the baby powder and sweet scent, and his knees buckled. But his daughter was nowhere to be found.

Greer stood at the door. "She's with my friend Tori," she whispered. "She babysits her some when I'm working and she doesn't have a shift at the hospital. Sometimes another friend, Cindy, watches her."

Locke didn't know what to say first. He was flooded. Overwhelmed.

"How could you, Greer? How could you hide this from me? Do this to me?" With every question, his voice rose and his pulse rocketed.

"Locke, you said you didn't want children."

He collapsed into the rocking chair, dropping his head into his hands. He had said that and he'd meant it at the time, but he didn't have a flesh-and-blood child to see or touch or talk to. Now he did and that changed things.

He was furious for the betrayal. Terrified of what this now meant. How was he supposed to be a dad—not just a dad but a good one? Yeah, he'd told Greer that he didn't want kids. Yeah, his excuse was his on-the-go lifestyle not being conducive to children. But that wasn't the deep-down-inside reason. That reason was too embarrassing to reveal. Especially to the woman he'd wanted to pledge his life to. It was too raw, making him too vulnerable. It would have shown her who he really was and she would have left him. She'd left him, anyway, in the end, but not for the truth. Not for the real reason he didn't want to be a father.

The truth was, Locke couldn't handle disappointing and failing one more person. Most definitely not his own flesh and blood. He'd been a screw-up his whole life. It was easier to let Greer believe the superficial excuse.

"You said you didn't want them, either, but here you are. A mama. You didn't put her up for adoption. You changed gears and didn't allow me to change them. That's not fair."

Greer sighed. "No, it's not. And that has crossed my mind several times in the past few months. I even picked up the phone to call you…

but I didn't. And I can't change it now. I don't know where we go from here."

Locke wasn't sure, either. His biggest fear had come true in two seconds flat. Underneath that fear, though, was a powerful need to see his baby. It pulled at him like gravity. He may not have wanted a kid, but he had one now. And he wanted her.

"I want to see her."

"It's the middle of the night. She's asleep."

Locke worked his jaw, studied the room. "I want to see her first thing this morning, Greer."

Greer exhaled a shaky breath, but she nodded. "I understand if you want to leave now."

She understood nothing. "No, I can't leave. As much as I want to." He needed to clear his head. Think things out. There was so much to process and his mind was going billions of miles a minute. "Because some crazy is out there trying to kill you. So, I'll be staying." He paused beside her. "Make no mistake, though. It has *nothing* to do with how I feel about you." She'd hidden a human being from him and if he hadn't come to town, he still wouldn't know! That was unfair no matter what he'd said about having or not having kids. It didn't matter how terrified he was knowing he was a father. This was his baby. His. Baby. "But you're the mother of my child. So, I won't let anything happen to you. For *my* child's sake."

At the door, Greer sniffed. A sliver of him wanted to go and comfort her. But he was aching inside and needed to be alone.

"I'm taking the couch." He marched down the hall and into the living room.

He fell onto the sofa, face in a throw pillow. Greer's bedroom door quietly clicked closed and everything he felt, everything he'd missed out on, every slice of her betrayal, broke through and washed out his eyes on to the sagging couch.

When the alarm went off at 6:00 a.m., Greer rolled over and turned it off. She hadn't slept a wink. After Deputy Crisp fingerprinted the window, she'd spent most of the night sobbing and begging God to help her figure this out. She'd never seen Locke so angry, though he had every right to be. Every right to hate her, to be disgusted. But he'd never understand her reasons. Locke wouldn't believe he'd ever resent them and walk out one day. Her own dad probably hadn't even thought that at first. One day it *would* happen. Locke never looked much to the future. He lived in the now. That was his way. She'd done what she thought was best. Right or wrong. She couldn't take it back.

Now that Locke knew, Greer feared what he

might do. What if he tried to take Lin from her? And do what with her? Take her to live in campers while he chased storms? Just toss her in a car seat with a toy camera as he raced with twisters? Hardly. But he was extremely impulsive to say the least, so Greer couldn't be sure what he would or wouldn't do.

When he'd shown up at her house after rescuing her again, she had been terrified, but then he'd taken her and held her against him. All the comfort and warmth she'd needed, he'd provided. His tenderness had been overwhelming. Twice he'd risked his life for her.

But now his protection was only due to the fact they shared a child. Any tender feelings he had were gone. Better that way, anyway.

That wasn't the only terrifying thing sending her heart into arrhythmia. Locke was right when he said a killer wanted her dead. Somehow, the man in the maintenance uniform had discovered where she lived and she wasn't safe. Greer had barely gotten free from his grasp a second time. Barely made it outside. If Locke hadn't been there—again—she might not have made it at all. And what if Lin had been home? Her baby wasn't safe, either. This guy wasn't going to stop coming for her.

Today was going to be a long day. They had to find him. Put him away. It was the only way

Greer and Lin would be safe. But before she could get to work and do her job, she had to take Locke to see Lin.

After cleaning up, she found him sitting at the kitchen table, eyes red-rimmed and hair disheveled. Didn't look like he'd slept, either. She wasn't sure if she was going to get more heat or if he'd blown his top and now would be less harsh. Either way, she'd take whatever dish he served up, whether hot or cold, and eat it without complaint.

"What time does she wake up?" he asked quietly.

"About now. I'll call Tori and let her know we're coming. Do—do you want anything to eat or drink?"

"I don't want anything, Greer," he murmured. "Just my daughter."

She swallowed the ache in her throat and nodded, then went into her bedroom to call Tori—the only person in town who knew everything. Tori had been her best friend since third grade. When she reentered the kitchen, Locke had changed clothes and looked like he'd shaved. A duffel bag hung over his shoulder. The fact he'd freshened up to meet his nine-month-old baby girl sent a wave of warmth and grief through her.

He silently followed her outside.

"Do you want to ride together?"

"I do not."

"Okay," she mumbled. "Tori lives on a farm on the edge of town. She homesteads." Now she was nervously babbling. "Just…follow me."

As she neared Tori's farm, her stomach knotted, and she felt like she might throw up. She pulled up behind Tori's car. Locke was behind her in his Ford F-150. He followed her to the screened-in door at the side of the house. Tori met them at the door.

"This is Locke."

"Hey," Locke said, devoid of his typical charm and friendliness.

"Nice to meet you. She's…she's in her high chair."

They entered the kitchen; the smell of toast and coffee permeated the room. Greer's heart swelled when she saw Lin sitting in a wooden high chair with a few rice puffs on her tray. "Hi, baby girl," Greer cooed.

Lin looked up, gave her that wide grin and banged on her tray, squealing. Nothing made Greer feel more loved and wanted. Locke hung back. His bravado, his anger, gone. He almost seemed nervous. Shy. Uncertain. Greer lifted Lin from the high chair and kissed her chubby cheek. "Mama missed you, baby girl. Did you have fun with Miss Tori?" She kissed her again and slowly brought her to Locke.

"I have some work down in the root cellar. I'll be there if you need me." Tori left them alone, and Greer brought Lin to him.

"She's going through stranger anxiety so she may not warm up very fast," Greer said.

"And do you know what that feels like, Greer? To be a stranger to your own child?" he whispered. "Does she have a name? I don't even know my daughter's name." Anguish swept through his tone, and regret panged in her heart.

"Locklin, meet Stormie Lin. But she goes by Lin. L-i-n."

Moisture formed in his eyes. "Lin," he whispered. "Stormie Lin," he whispered again. He looked at Greer, blinked back the moisture. His blue eyes were bright. Clear. "What's her last name?"

Greer's dream had always been to carry his last name. Her daughter should as well. "On the birth certificate it's Gallagher. But around here, she's Lin Montgomery."

Locke sniffed, studied Lin. "At least you gave her my name legally. Thank you."

A thank-you. Greer bit her lower lip. Locke reached out, hesitated, then touched Lin's cheek. "Hey," he said with a soft baby-talk tone. "Hey, Lin."

She peered at her daddy, into identical eyes, with a somber expression. He tickled under her chin. "Do you know who I am?" He became more cheerful as if working to draw a smile. "I'm your...daddy." His voice choked with emotion on the word. "Can you say 'daddy'?" he asked.

Lin wrapped her pudgy hand around his finger on her chin and blew spit bubbles.

Locke chuckled, and she squealed.

"Can I...hold her?" he asked.

"We can try, yes." Greer slowly passed Lin to Locke. "Go see your daddy, baby girl. It's okay."

Lin swiveled toward Greer but allowed Locke to take her in his arms. Greer had been in those arms many times. Surely, Lin would feel the strength and security in them, as Greer always had. The feeling of protection. She only hoped her baby girl would never have to live with those strong, safe arms leaving her.

Locke took her hand and kissed her baby knuckles. "Hey."

Bless him, he had no clue what to say or do, but his affection was clear. Burning bright in his eyes. "You are so lovely, little girl."

Greer turned and squeezed her eyes shut, holding back tears.

"Did you know that? Did you know you were so lovely?" he asked again.

Greer faced them, watched. Lin put her hand on his cheek and squeezed.

"Mmm…you got a grip there, kiddo." Locke laughed. "Good solid grip."

Greer chuckled, and Lin laughed with her.

"Well, she likes you."

"She should. I'm her dad," he said strongly. "I want to know everything, Greer. I want to know everything I missed. Because I've missed it all. You have to understand that, right?"

Greer bit back tears. "I didn't want us to be in your way. You'd just signed the two-year contract. I hadn't. You were working your way into your dream. And…"

"And what?"

How did she explain that she knew he'd end up abandoning them? He'd just argue with her. "And, I'm sorry." Sorry for this whole mess.

"Me, too." He rubbed Lin's soft cap of raven hair. "It curls when it's wet, doesn't it?" he asked.

"It does."

"So does mine." He grinned.

"I know," she whispered. "I'll tell you everything. Show you photos. Videos." Whatever he wanted. But that didn't make the fear go away. Seeing his gentleness didn't give her hope. Dad had been fun with her, too. When she was little, he'd called her *precious*. "But I have to go to work, Locke. A killer is out there, and you're right. I'm not safe until he's behind bars." She couldn't let Locke see how terrified she truly

was. He might try to take Lin away or something. She had to appear confident. Brave. In
control. But she had never felt more helpless and
out of control.

"New storm system coming in today. Around
two. I have to work, too, but I want all the time
I have with her. You owe me that."

"I know." But what about after? All the time
he had. Meaning he wasn't going to have a lifetime. Her anxiety ramped up and all she felt was
her own rejection. Same rejection Lin would feel
if Locke thought he could waltz in and out.

Lin wiggled in Locke's arms and reached for
the high chair.

"She wants her juice." Greer handed it to her.
"Let's go in the living room." She had about an
hour before she needed to be on her way to the
carnival. Interviews to conduct. A murder to investigate. She wasn't sure what scared her most
right now.

The killer or Locke.

THREE

Greer had changed into her deputy's uniform and walked through the carnival, watching closely. It was still early and quiet. Word spread fast, but it wouldn't keep patrons away for long. The storms wouldn't, either. While rain wasn't coming down now, it was hazy, gray and chilly.

Carnival employees were setting up, and the smell of funnel cakes and turkey legs wafted in the spring air and made Greer's stomach rumble. She hadn't been able to eat all morning. Locke had asked about labor. Birth. Lin's health. An arsenal of questions and she'd agreed to show him photo albums and videos later this afternoon, when she had a chance and when he was available. With storm systems came unpredictability, and his job wasn't nine-to-five.

"Hey, Greer." Deputy Adam Crisp met up with her by the lemonade stand. "You sleep okay after I left?" His blond hair was lighter than hers. His eyes steel-gray. He'd moved from Decatur,

Alabama, a little over a year ago. Both new to the Jenkins County Sheriff's Department, they'd become fast friends. He was like a brother to her and checked up on her often.

"Sure."

He tossed a skeptical glance her way. "I drove by a few times before Garrison took my shift. Noticed your out-of-town friend didn't leave."

Well, that appeared a bit unsavory. She was shocked he hadn't run the plates. Maybe he had. "How far did y'all get last night?" she asked, changing the subject.

"We got the files from the carnival managers and owners—Rudy and Jenna Dennsion. Nice enough. Helpful enough." They walked toward the employee campers. Was he here? Did he see her? Would he try to attack her again? She'd be ready, but it didn't give her racing heart any measure of peace. *Lord, help me and protect me today.* "We talked with the workers on either side of Flip's camper, but they were setting up games and stands. Didn't see anything. Hear anything."

So they said.

"What about the maintenance workers that work this carnival?"

"We talked to two out of three." He flipped his notepad. "Frandel Modine and a Carlie Castle."

Well, it wasn't a female who attacked her. "And the third?"

"Ray Don Chatham." Adam's mouth turned grim. "He couldn't be found last night. But we'll track him down. He fits your description. Beard. Mustache. Wide nose. Wish you had more."

"It was pitch-black and it happened pretty fast." They approached Flip's camper. "Did Frandel have an alibi for last night?" she asked.

"He was with Carlie Castle. They're a thing."

Maybe she covered for him, then. "What did you find out on Flip Bomer?"

Adam tripped over an extension cord and growled. "I hate carnivals."

Greer chuckled. "Same." But there was a time when she'd loved them. One in particular stood out, but she wasn't thinking about Locke right now.

"Not much more on Flip. Hoping to get some answers this morning." They entered Flip's quarters, and Greer shuddered. Seeing that monster. The knife. What she'd gone through last night.

"How is Lin?" Adam asked.

"Good. She stayed with Tori. Probably going to let her stay there and elsewhere until we figure out what's going on. Safer if he returns."

Adam nodded and slipped on a pair of latex gloves. "What're you looking for here? We already combed the place last night."

"I don't know. I just want another look." Flip wasn't a tidy person. "If someone had a beef with him, then maybe there's some kind of evidence. I doubt he was a random victim. We need to find out if he had enemies. Something." They continued their search. "Nothing of worth in here. Let's see if the maintenance worker has returned home."

Adam led the way to an RV that was a little larger than Flip's. He knocked on the door. "Jenkins County Sheriff's Department." Rustling sounded.

The door opened, and Greer held her breath. What if she was looking at the man who had tried to kill her last night? "I'm Deputy Montgomery," she said, "and this is Deputy Crisp."

"Like apple crisp?" the guy asked and laughed. Bloodshot eyes. Dressed in a white tank top and low-hanging jeans—he was fit. Facial hair. Wide nose, and even the same height and weight. But she couldn't say confidently.

"Ray Don Chatham?"

"Maybe."

The smell of liquor wafted out of the camper, nearly knocking Greer back. Had this guy been on a bender all night? If so, he couldn't be the attacker. He hadn't smelled of booze. But after the attack on her at home, he may have headed to a local tavern or bar. "We're here about Flip Bomer. Were you friends?"

Ray Don laughed and coughed. One too many

cigarettes. "Flip didn't have friends. He was a lying, cheating, blackmailing piece of rotting flesh. No one is going to be crying over his death or willing to help you find his killer. He's a hero."

Lovely.

"Where were you last night between the hours of seven p.m. and three a.m.?" Adam asked.

"Found me a nice little place to have a drink. Southern Comfort."

Local tavern on the edge of town. "Anyone be able to corroborate that?" Greer asked.

"What?"

"Anyone be able to back you up?" Greer re-stated.

"I don't know. I drink alone." He grinned.

"You said Flip was a blackmailer." Greer glanced at Adam. "He blackmail you?"

Ray Don lit up a cigarette; the smoke billowed and he squinted an eye while he inhaled a deep drag. He blew it out. "If he had anything on me, he would have. You should talk to Jewel."

"Where can we find this Jewel?" Adam asked.

"Far side. Blue-and-white camper." He pointed to the west side of the camp, then closed his door.

"Can you identify him as your attacker?" Adam asked.

That was the thing. She couldn't. It was possible that whoever killed Flip and attacked her might not be a maintenance worker at all. He could have impersonated one. If an employee saw him entering Flip's camper, then they'd assume it was one of their guys. In actuality, it could have been a game worker, a hot dog stand attendant, clown, juggler, anyone. It would be smart to slide into a uniform and throw off anyone who may have witnessed him slinking around the carnival and employee campgrounds.

"No. Let's check Southern Comfort, see if his alibi is corroborated. If so, I think we may be dealing with someone who lifted a uniform off of one the carnies. If it isn't…we haul him in."

"I agree," Adam said.

"But first, let's chat with this Jewel person," Greer said as she and Adam trekked through the muddy ground to Jewel's camper. "What do you think of this whole blackmail thing?"

Adam shrugged. "I think we're dealing with all sorts of shady characters and anything could happen. I hope we nail the guy before the week ends. If Ray Don doesn't pan out as our lead and we don't find any others, they'll be free to pack up and move on."

Greer was afraid of that. The only one who could identify this guy was Greer. If he wanted to move on with the carnival, he'd have to try and finish what he started. She shivered.

"You cold?"

"Yeah. Sure." They made it to the blue-and-white camper, and Greer knocked. A young woman in her early twenties in a flimsy robe opened the door.

"Can I help you?"

"Are you Jewel?" Adam asked.

"I am."

"Got a last name?" Greer asked.

"Pharelli."

They introduced themselves and relayed Ray Don's words. Jewel sighed. "Flip was a real piece of work. Ray Don is right. No one liked Flip. How can I help you?"

"Was he blackmailing you?" Greer asked.

"No," she said, biting her lower lip and refusing to make eye contact.

"Look, we're after who murdered Flip and attacked me. Twice. But we need to know."

Jewel wiped wet eyes. "He knew I had a relationship with someone in the carnival. Someone married. It was brief and a big mistake on my part. But I need this job."

"Was the man you had a short relationship with also being blackmailed?" Greer asked.

She nodded. "Breaking it off didn't change it, either. I mean, that's not why I stopped seeing him. It was wrong. So wrong. And even after, Flip kept asking for money. We kept paying. But we didn't kill him."

"Did he have evidence proving the affair or just knowledge?"

Jewel nodded again. "Photos. I don't know where he kept them, though. His place has been tossed on more than one occasion. But he keeps on keeping on. I'm not sad he's dead."

Seemed to be the consensus. "I'm going to need the name of the man." It wasn't a woman who had tried to end her life. Could have been the guy she was trying to protect.

"I'm not giving you that. And you can't make me."

No, they couldn't. But she could appeal to her sense of sympathy. "I'm a single mama. The killer tried to take me away from my baby girl. I need to catch this guy. Please help me."

Jewel sighed. "Rudy Dennison."

The carnival manager. Well, this made things more interesting. He'd have everything to lose if this information came out. The carnival had been around for over fifty years, opened and operated by the Wheeler family. Jenna Dennison's maiden name. Her family. If she found out about Rudy, he would be out in the cold. Jewel, too.

Adam glanced at Greer, and he barely nodded. They were on the same page. "We'll be discreet since you cooperated, Miss Pharelli," Adam said.

"Thank you." She closed the door on them.

"If this guy would blackmail the manager and owner-by-marriage, then what wouldn't he do? And who hasn't he done it to?" Greer asked. This might go deeper and take longer than she originally suspected.

"I was thinking the same thing. Any one of 'em could have done it. And any one of 'em could be covering for him, especially if they were also being blackmailed," Adam said as they strode toward the manager's RV. "If you need me to bunk on your couch a few days, let me know," Adam said. "I don't like this guy out in the open. Here."

Neither did Greer. Even now she felt like those dead eyes were on her, watching, lurking. Waiting for her to be alone so he could try and finish what he started. "I'm good. Really."

"How long is your out-of-town friend staying?"

Greer's cheeks heated. He'd met Locke last night. He couldn't have forgotten his name. She sighed. "Not long." Too long. She didn't want to discuss it with Adam. Or anyone.

"I get the back-off vibe. So, I will." He knocked on the Dennisons' RV door.

No answer.

"Probably somewhere in the fair," Greer said. "Let's talk to some other workers and maybe we'll catch up with him." They made their rounds. Most workers didn't want to get involved. Was it because they'd been blackmailed and wanted to keep it a secret or did they simply want to keep their noses out of the whole thing? No one seemed worried they might be next on the list to die. It appeared Flip was a premeditated target. And Greer had been in the wrong place at the wrong time.

After a few hours, patrons had arrived at the fair, but not many since school was still in session. A field trip was coming on Monday. At around 1:00, her phone rang.

Cindy Woolridge.

Greer agreed to meet her at the Blue Bass café on Main Street. She needed a favor anyway. Greer left Adam at the fair and drove to the small café on the square. She parallel-parked and entered to the smell of fried fish, garlicky dishes and fresh homemade coconut pie.

She found Cindy and Michael—her husband—in a booth near the corner.

Michael stood to greet her with a side hug. "We placed your order."

"Oh, good, thanks."

Cindy grabbed her hand as she sat across from them. "I can't believe this. A murder in our town!" She clutched her chest, and Michael put his arm around her.

"I know." Greer's insides swished around,

leaving her nauseated, but not eating would only make her worse. If she was going to catch this killer, she needed strength.

"Any leads since earlier this morning?" Cindy asked. "I've talked with the mayor and Sheriff Wright. Minus you being in the wrong place at the wrong time, they feel it's an isolated incident."

Greer rubbed her temples. "I think they're correct in assuming that, but we won't know more until we do more investigating." She relayed all she could, which wasn't much.

"Well, thank the good Lord for having an old friend in town to be nearby and help you." Cindy eyed her, and the questions about Locke drilled into her.

Michael said, "You know you can always come stay with us. Us Alabama boys know how to shoot." His teasing lightened the mood.

"That's generous. Really. But I don't know if he's going to come after me again, and the last thing I want to do is put you or your boys at risk." She patted her side. "And us Alabama girls know how to shoot, also."

The bell jingled and Greer glanced around to see Locke enter the café. She scooched farther down in the booth, concealing herself.

Cindy gave her a quizzical expression.

She couldn't think about Locke right now. She

needed help with Lin. "I don't want Lin in danger, either, so I need a favor."

"Name it," Cindy said.

Greer shot a look to the counter, where Locke sat with a soft drink. Looking lonely. Lost. How was all of this going to play out?

Locke ordered a cherry cola and toyed with the straw paper. He didn't have much of an appetite and had been more unfocused than usual. He'd given the team's lunch orders to the guy behind the counter and swiveled back and forth on the stool.

This morning had been a roller coaster ride. His anger had propelled him forward, but once he'd reached the farmhouse and gone inside, he'd turned clammy. His nerves got the best of him. Locke had rarely been around babies. Never even fed one or changed a diaper. So many questions had whipped through his mind. Questions like—what if he wasn't a good dad? What if Lin didn't like him? But then she was in his arms, and it was like the storm had been swept up into the sky and the atmosphere became warm and sunny. Locke had looked into his daughter's eyes and knew right then that there was no storm he wouldn't brave, no wall he wouldn't scale, no bullet he wouldn't take to protect her, to make sure she had everything she ever wanted and deserved.

He'd never experienced anything like it. But what if he failed her later on?

And Greer—Greer had not only named their daughter after their love for storms, but also after Locklin himself. That had undone something in him. Why would she be that considerate but not inform him she'd been pregnant? It didn't make sense. While it was thoughtful of her, it didn't make him any less angry at her for betraying him, not giving him his right to be a dad—even if he was destined to be horrible at it.

He'd been cut to the quick.

Now he felt hollow. Still angry. Still unable to forgive her. But confused. He wasn't sure what the next step was. He only knew he couldn't walk away from his daughter.

"Greer, did you want that burger well-done?" the cook called from behind the counter. "I can't ever remember."

Locke spun around and met Greer's gaze. Uncertainty. Fear. Dread. It all pulsed there. The last thing he'd ever wanted was for her to fear him, dread him or feel uncertain about him. But they were in uncharted waters.

She didn't move. Blink.

Locke turned back around. "Medium well. She wants it medium well." He slipped off the stool and wandered over. Not even sure why. He wanted distance from her. To lick his wounds. But Greer had been like gravity since the day he'd laid eyes on her outside their college classroom. Guess she still had a pull. Even if he didn't like it.

"Hey," she murmured.

"Hey." He looked at the woman and man in the seat across from Greer. White collar met blue collar.

Greer cleared her throat. "This is Michael and Cindy Woolridge. Cindy is the executive director for the chamber of commerce and Michael manages B and P Construction Company."

Michael shook Locke's hand. Nice firm grip. "Good to meet you."

Cindy smiled. "Please, have a seat."

Greer's cheeks flamed, but she scooted over, unwilling to make a scene and admit the truth. Doubtful these folks knew he was the baby daddy—the uninformed baby daddy. He clamped down on the fresh wave of anger—of hurt. He quietly sat on the edge of the booth.

"You must be the friend who rescued Greer. Twice. We were telling her how blessed she was to have you nearby," Cindy said.

Locke gave a tight smile. He wasn't opposed to faith. Locke had known the joy of giving his heart to God when he was small. But as he became an adult, things weren't quite so black-and-white.

"You said you wanted a favor. I'm guessing you need us to keep Lin when Tori goes back to work," Cindy said and added another lemon to her drink.

"Yes, I do." Greer's hand trembled and Locke's first reaction was to grab it and calm her. But before he made contact, he balled his fist and forced it in his lap. He wasn't her comforter. He wasn't even sure he was her friend anymore. Though, less than twenty-four hours ago, he'd wanted to be. Friends didn't betray one another. Friends didn't keep secrets. Didn't hide things. Friends could be trusted.

"With these crazy storms, I'm not doing much on-site work. Too wet. Which means I'm on extra Dad duty," Michael said. "Whatever you need, let us know."

Greer teared up. "Thank y'all so much. This helps a bunch."

Looked like this town cared a lot about her. He'd been wondering if she was all alone in this, but he guessed not.

Her phone rang. She answered. "Deputy Montgomery." Her shoulders tensed. "I'll be right there." She hung up. "I have to go. They found another body. Possibly another carnival worker."

Locke's heart jumped in his throat. "I thought this was about that Flip guy only. What is going on?"

"I have no idea. More blackmailing? I can't say until I get over there and know more."

Greer nudged him to move and let her out of the booth. Part of him wanted to block her. Keep her from going into danger. What if the killer was hiding and tried to attack her when she was on the scene? "How do you know you'll be safe?"

"It's daylight. I won't be the only one there, and I'm a trained officer."

Locke scooted from the booth and let her out.

"Saturday night okay?" she asked Cindy. "Tori has to be back on duty at the hospital for the night shift."

"Of course. We'll bring her to you at church," Cindy said.

They said their goodbyes and Locke followed her out. "Can I go with you?"

"For what? If you wanted to be a bodyguard, you should have gone to work for your cousin's private security company." She huffed and unlocked the door to her patrol car.

"I don't like that a killer is out there and going on a rampage. One that involves—" his lips pursed and he glanced away "—the mother of my child."

She slid into her seat and buckled up. "The mother of your child can take care of herself."

"Didn't seem that way last night." Was he trying to pick a fight? Maybe. But it ate at him. He was furious with her and—and scared for her. Not because of Lin. Because it was Greer.

"I have to go." She didn't wait for him to step away. She pulled from the curb.

His gut screamed this wasn't a cut-and-dried carny case. Screamed that Greer was in more danger than she even knew. But she wouldn't listen to that. Not without proof. He'd just have to watch out for her himself.

How was the question? He had a job to do. He wasn't here on vacation. The storms wouldn't hold off for him. His research team members were all cool guys, but they were working on a grant, and if they didn't produce something they might not get another one, and Locke needed them to get one to keep him in a steady job with steady income, especially now that he knew he had a daughter to provide for.

But presently their safety was his major concern.

The warning in his gut burned like fire. No way he was letting her go to that crime scene without him. Not when he feared trouble was around the bend.

FOUR

Greer pulled up to Southern Comfort tavern and parked at the edge of the lot. A crowd had already gathered like the gray thunderheads above. Another storm brewing.

Greer's heart had a storm brewing as well. A killer to catch. Trying to stay alive. Relying on others to tend her daughter. Greer was the parent and she missed Lin so much. She already felt guilty for the amount of time she spent working her day job and side jobs, but what choice did she have? If she was going to buy formula, food and diapers then Greer had to work. But the facts didn't relieve the guilt that half of Lin's time was spent with someone else caring for her. Now wasn't the time to cry about it. It wasn't the time to wonder about what Locke might do or try to do.

Adam met her as she entered the smoky tavern. Just after lunch and not everyone inside was having a burger. Whispers abounded. "What do we got?"

"I just got here. Talked to Wally." He pointed to the owner, who was dealing drinks behind the bar. Tired eyes. Friendly smile. "Said he didn't notice the body this morning when he came in to prep for the lunch crowd. Tyrell found him when he carried out the trash. So, I reckon somewhere between eleven and noon, the guy was killed."

"Or dumped," Greer interjected. But why dump a body in a public place?

"Maybe. You know this is the same bar the missing maintenance worker from last night was drinking in. Wally says he could have been here, but it was packed like sardines with people from all over the county here to see the live band. It's going to be tough to confirm his alibi. We'll keep asking though."

Greer could haul in Ray Don, but without witnesses or alibis, they would get nowhere. "Any cameras?"

"Not a one."

Great. "Let's look at our victim and see what we see." She took the lead and went out the side door, where the surrounding area, including the enclosed dumpsters, was cordoned off with crime-scene tape. "I'm on crime-scene photo duty, too." She handed Adam her kit with the numbered placards to place by any evidence.

They donned their booties and latex gloves. Greer pulled her hair into a Jenkins County ball cap. The wind picked up, blowing the scent of rotting garbage and liquor through the air. Greer crinkled her nose.

She worked at taking photos of the actual scene. Tyrell stood off at a distance talking to Deputy Garrison. Greer tiptoed around the back of the large, rusted green Dumpster. The victim was lying faceup. He hadn't gone easy. Greer kneeled. "His denim jacket is damp. Not from blood."

"Hasn't rained this morning," Adam said.

Wally hadn't found him because he was hidden. Behind the Dumpster. "I think he was murdered last night. Coroner will be able to tell us more." Lot of blood. But not enough washed away from the rain that had come in last night. "Anyone call him?"

"Sheriff did. He's on his way." Adam kneeled. "Looks like multiple stab wounds." Like Flip. He winced. "Same knife that killed Flip Bomer?"

"Don't know." Greer placed a numbered card on the ground and took several more pics of their vic. "But he's not local."

Adam carefully lifted his denim jacket and drew out a wallet. "Timothy Maynard. Thirty-four. Georgia license."

"Carny?"

"I'm guessing," Adam said and replaced the wallet. "Unless he has family in the band and he came to visit, but that's not likely. Let's talk to Tyrell."

"After we finish here. I don't want the new rain washin' out what we have. Bag his hands and feet." She'd already taken the photos of the body. "You think he might be in the blackmail business with Flip if he's a carny?"

"I don't know," Adam said. "I'm not sure what in the world is going on at that carnival. Other than some kind of blackmail war." Adam frowned. "I don't like you staying home alone, Greer."

"I'm capable of taking care of myself, but thanks."

"I worry about you is all."

"I appreciate it." A figure caught her eye and she did a double take. "You have got to be kidding me," she muttered and growled under her breath. Locke was heading straight for the crime scene tape. Straight for her. "Can you finish up here? I have all the photos we need."

Adam followed her line of sight. "Out-of-town friend?" His voice was a bit stern. But then Adam was protective of Greer. Might as well be honest. Adam already knew—it was in his eyes. There was no hiding it, not when Lin looked exactly like Locke.

"He's Lin's father. He's here for a week."

"Yeah, well where was the deadbeat when you were having her? When you were taking job number two and three?" Ice laced his voice. He wasn't being fair, but only because he didn't know that Greer had kept Lin a secret.

"It's complicated."

She ignored his grunt and strode to the edge of the scene, then slipped under the tape. "What are you doing here? Because last I checked, you ordered lunch already and you don't drink."

"Maybe I started," he returned with a whole lot of smart aleck in his voice.

"Ha-ha. Seriously, why are you here?"

"I was worried, okay? Sue me."

Greer sighed, unsure how she felt. The fact he was here keeping silent guard slid into fear-laden places and brought solace, but it had nothing to do with Greer and everything to do with Lin. With keeping the mother of his child safe. Still honorable. Still stung, if only slightly.

"Well, I'm fine. Doing my job. And I'm not alone." She pointed at Adam, who was now talking to Tyrell, but she felt his eyes on her. Or someone's eyes. Suddenly, her skin turned cold, leaving goose bumps. Maybe Greer wasn't as alone as she thought.

"What is it?" Locke asked.

"Nothing." She shrugged off the eerie notion

that the killer was present. Lurking. "We have enough spectators, Locke. Go back to work. Storm's coming in a few hours. Maybe sooner."

He smirked.

It messed with her heart's equilibrium. Of course, he'd know a storm was coming. It amused him, she knew. There wasn't anything he'd taught her that she'd forgotten. Including his stubbornness, which was off the charts and only equal to his insane impulsiveness. "I have to go back to work." She stalked back to Adam, who was interviewing Tyrell.

"I usually smoke behind the trash Dumpsters, but I'm telling you I think that sight scared the nicotine out of me for good, you know?" Tyrell said.

"I hear ya," Adam replied. "So, Timothy was here last night?"

"Drinking on the stool 'til way after midnight."

Adam turned to Greer. "Do we have a picture of Ray Don to show him?"

"I don't think so." Her phone rang. She answered. "Jimmy?" Why was the dispatcher calling?

"Hey, Greer. We got a 911 call from your neighbor, Ms. Hatter. She said someone broke into your house. She saw him. Thought I'd call you first."

Again? "Is he in there now?"

"She said he ran."

"I'm on my way!" Greer hit the end button. "Someone was in my home. I gotta go."

"I can come with you."

"You're better off finishing up here." Locke hadn't left and would no doubt insert himself into the situation.

"And if he comes back?"

No doubt, at some point he would. "I'll be okay." She jogged under the tape and Locke came up beside her.

"Greer, what happened?" Locke's concern was loud, intense.

"Intruder was in the house. I'm on my way there."

"Why don't you ride with me? We can come back for your car later."

"No. I'm on duty. I have my patrol car." She could speed. Get there faster.

"Well, I'm following you back to the house. End of story. I told you this guy wasn't going to stop. I knew in my gut something was wrong." In his tropical blue eyes, she saw fear. Something she'd never seen there before but it was easily identifiable.

She flipped on her lights and raced home with Locke right behind.

Ms. Hatter paced her front yard. Greer thanked God that she hadn't been harmed.

It started to sprinkle.

"Greer! Oh, sweet Greer!" she called as she hobbled over and they went underneath the porch to stay dry. "I was so scared. I came by to bring you a cake, and when I knocked on the door I saw him."

"What did he look like?"

Ms. Hatter clutched her chest. "He had on a black jacket with a hood and a ski mask. I thought I was dead, I did. He ran through the living room and out your patio door when I screamed. I ran back to my house and called the police."

"I'm relieved he didn't hurt you, Ms. Hatter. I'm so sorry." What if he had hurt her? Stabbed her? Sweet Ms. Hatter was always kind and willing to keep Lin, but she had Parkinson's and wasn't able to hold Lin for long periods of time. Instead, she brought over many meals and little happies for Lin. Bless her heart.

"Don't you be sorry, hon." She hugged her tight. "I'll keep praying for you."

"Thank you." Greer unlocked the front door and entered the house. The kitchen was intact. The living room had been turned upside down, but not destroyed. What was he after?

"Greer," Locke said, standing frozen in the

living room. "If he was trying to silence you for witnessing a murder, then why would he come here and toss this place?"

Greer wondered the same thing. A cold finger slid up her back. "I don't know."

"Maybe he thinks you took Flip's blackmail stash."

"I'd put that into evidence. At the station."

Locke nodded and traipsed to the corner where her desk was. He'd really destroyed that area. "Greer, did you take your laptop to work with you this morning?"

"No." Dread pooled in her gut as she surveyed her desk. The drawers had all been emptied, the top of it ransacked.

"It's gone. Check and see if anything else is, too."

Greer rummaged through her desk and drawers. "My photo-editing software I downloaded to the computer is gone."

"Why would he steal that?"

Good question. Greer had no clue.

A slash of lightning bolted across the front windows of Greer's house. Thunder rumbled. Rain pounded the roof as if demanding it open up. Only the middle of the afternoon, but the house was shadowy and Greer stood with trembling hands. Locke wanted to steady them in his, but he was still angry with her for hiding a baby from him. Fear was running a close second to anger. He'd had little time to process any of this with the attacks and having to monitor storms.

But underneath all the anger and fear, a resolve rose. No one was going to lay a hand on one single hair of Greer's head.

"I'm staying here," Locke said. "Indefinitely. You're not safe. Thirty-minute drive-bys aren't good enough. And I know a town this small doesn't have the funds to provide around-the-clock care."

Greer threaded her fingers through her hair and breathed deep. She had to know he was right. "It just looks bad."

"I don't care what nosy busybodies think. They'd do the same thing if their lives were in danger. Besides, I imagine the whole town knows you have something going on with that deputy guy."

"Adam?" Greer frowned.

Whatever his name was. Locke was a man. And one man knew when another man was into a woman. By the way Greer hugged him and seemed familiar with him, he had his suspicions that they were an item, or working their way to be one. Which made sense if Greer wanted to be with someone who loved being in law enforcement as much as she did. That wasn't Locke. It was the first place they'd met—criminal justice classes. The first topic of their conversations. Greer had been excited to be there studying. Anticipated the day she wore the uniform. And Locke had kept silent about his feelings of being forced into the career by family pressures and a big dose of guilt.

It wasn't until much later, when he'd shared the truth, but Greer had already offered her whole heart to him. It hadn't mattered to her that he didn't want to eventually be a cop—or a dad. But apparently it had.

"I mean, date him if you want. It's whatever." He didn't want to talk about it. "You're free to see anyone. I'm only concerned about Lin." That wasn't completely true, but he needed to protect himself. "So, he'll just have to get over the fact that the father of your child is sticking around a while." What happened when it was time to pack up and leave? What if the killer hadn't been caught? What about Lin? Too many what-ifs. "What's the next step?"

Greer's phone rang and she answered. "Hey, Adam."

Of course. Surely, he was checking in on her. Making sure she was safe.

"He is."

Asking about the baby daddy. She talked a few more minutes, hung up then answered another call. Locke made a pot of coffee. He had nowhere to be until the supercell storm rolled in later this evening. Greer finally entered the kitchen. "Smells good."

"What did he have to say?" He poured her a cup and brought it to her at the kitchen table. "You can confide the information to me. I'm not going to the papers or a gossip magazine." After pouring himself a cup, he sat across from her at the kitchen table while the rain fell like a curtain outside, blurring everything in a muted gray.

"Our victim is a carny. Tim Maynard. Goes by 'Tiny.'"

"Tiny Tim. Are you being serious right now?" Locke chuckled over his sip of coffee.

"I wouldn't lie about that."

No, she'd just lie about having a baby together. The tension in the room built at Mach speed and they drank their cups of coffee in silence.

Finally, Locke spoke. "Do they know if the same guy killed him who killed Flip Bomer?"

"Multiple stab wounds, which match the same kind of blade used on Flip, according to the coroner. No news yet on the trace evidence. We've asked for a rush considering the carnival is only in town a week, but that isn't a guarantee."

"Do you need to go back to the carnival? Interview people?" Locke asked.

"That was the other thing." Greer scowled.

"Sheriff called right after. Says since I've been a 'victim' more than once—" she used air quotes "—he feels that my investigating is a conflict of interest. So... I'm being kept abreast."

Greer was one of the most headstrong women he knew. "You're just gonna back down, then? Do as you're told?"

She snorted and stood. "What do you think?"

"I think you should call me Watson and expect me to be by your side in every off-duty search or investigation."

"And what if that takes place during a storm? One that needs your expertise."

That was a good question. "We'll cross that bridge when we get there." Seemed like they had dozens of bridges to cross. All rickety and unstable. "In the meantime, if you aren't going back out to the carnival, I'd like to see my daughter again." It was strange to be so afraid of such a little person—afraid of letting her down—and yet he wanted to be near her at the same time. Crazy.

Greer nodded and scanned the disaster. "I'll do this tonight."

"I'll help you." He couldn't very well sit here and watch her do it while he did zip. Which brought him back around to later, when he was out photographing. Greer couldn't be here alone.

He wouldn't let her. He grabbed his keys off the kitchen counter.

"You don't have to do that, Locke. But I appreciate it." The dejectedness and exhaustion in her voice tugged at him, and he closed the distance between them and embraced her, immediately regretting his impulsive decision because having her in his arms unleashed a whirlwind of emotion he told himself he was not going to feel, especially after she'd dropped the bomb on him.

Greer didn't wrench away. For a second she bristled, but then she melded against him as if trying to draw some of his own strength into herself. Petite. Delicate. Even fragile. Yet fierce and strong. Brave. What kind of woman took on such a challenging job while trying to raise a baby alone? No family. Her mama had just recently passed. But here she was. Still standing, moving forward, fighting to live another day. How could one man admire a woman who he was absolutely miffed at? Could be that it wasn't so much anger as heartache. Frustration. Rejection. Confusion.

And yet he held on tighter. "It's going to be okay, Greer. Somehow. Some way. It will. Let's go see Lin. That will make things better." He'd only seen his baby once, but there was no doubt that she was the sunshine who could bring hope to their cloud-filled day. He only hoped one day she wouldn't see him as gray clouds in her world.

"It will," she whispered and broke away. They grabbed their raincoats and rushed into the heavy rain and gales. Locke opened the truck door for her, then bolted to his side and cranked the engine. Inside, he had specialized gear on the console with satellite mapping and radars. The floorboards were littered with maps and papers.

"Sorry about the mess." He switched on a satellite and tracked the storm. "Storm'll be gone in about an hour or so."

Greer studied the monitor. "That's pretty cool equipment."

"It is." He shared with her some of what they'd been doing. "If the grant money comes through, I've been asked to sign on for another two years."

Greer stared out the window. Only the sound of the wipers slicing and squeaking across the windshield. "Is that what you want?"

It was until he'd come here. "I don't know what I want anymore. I feel caged."

Her head snapped up and she looked like she might fall to pieces. "Don't ever think I'm trying to cage you, Locke. That was the whole point in not telling you about Lin. I'd rather you go and be happy…and free than to try and do the 'right' thing."

Locke's words about being caged hadn't come

out right. Decisions had always been tough for him. He had to work at processing his way through them, and the more difficult, the more focus he lost. It was like being caged and then the cage rattling. Too much noise in his head. The decisions caged him, not his daughter. "I'd never shirk my responsibilities, Greer." Lin was a real-life reality. There was no running away even if a tiny sliver of his heart said it might be the best solution.

"I know," she said as he pulled into Tori's driveway. "But I didn't want you to have to choose between responsibilities and your freedom."

Greer thought Lin was a trap to him. She was so far off base, but then he had basically told Greer that years ago about kids in general. "Greer, I want to give you back pay at the very least."

"I don't want your money."

No, but she needed it. Now wasn't the time to argue. She was getting it, come hail or high water. "Will it be dinnertime for her?" It was nearly four. Didn't babies eat early?

"She usually eats dinner around five thirty, then a bottle before bed, around eight thirty. She loves to sleep." She glanced at Locke. "Unlike you."

Locke had too much energy to sleep but there

were many lazy Sunday afternoons Greer would curl up on a couch or a hammock—wherever they were—and take long naps. He envied her that. But the upside was, he had scads of photos of the sleeping beauty.

They rushed to the porch and Greer knocked.

Tori opened the door with Lin on her hip. Dressed in a one-piece blue outfit with little lambs, she was the cutest kid ever. She belonged on the cover of magazines. A little blue bow sat on the side of her thick head of hair. She bounced on Tori's hip, arms flailing as she laid eyes on her mama. Sheer excitement.

"Hey, baby girl," Greer cooed as she took her from Tori and they stepped inside. "You been a good little princess?"

"She's been happy as a pig in sunshine," Tori said. "I have some stuff to do, so I'm gonna make myself scarce."

Locke appreciated the privacy. Seemed like Tori was a great friend. "Hey, sweet girl," he said softly. Lin peered up at him. Would he ever get used to seeing his own reflection in her face? It was overwhelming.

Lin gave him a somber expression then grinned. Two top and two bottom teeth in a sea of gums and slobber. Slobber had never been more precious. For the next hour and a half, Locke played with his baby girl while Greer answered his endless questions. Then he fed her mixed vegetables and plums from jars, and while it smelled and looked like utter disgust, Lin licked up every bite with squeals that shifted and moved Locke's heart in places he didn't even know he had.

"It's bath time. Would you like to help with that?" Greer asked.

"Yeah, sure."

Bath time was equally as fun as dinnertime, only wetter. By seven, Lin was yawning and fussy, and reached for her mama. Greer hesitated.

"It's okay. I always wanted my mama when I was sleepy. Used to crawl up in her lap and let her play with my hair until I fell asleep." He handed off his daughter to Greer and she sat in one of Tori's rockers and hummed until Lin fell asleep. Greer placed her in a mesh baby bed in Tori's bedroom and closed the door.

"Monitors are on," she told Tori as she suddenly appeared.

"She'll be fine. I love having the little munchkin around. You need anything?"

"No, I guess we'll be going," Greer said and looked longingly toward Tori's room. To Lin. This separation must be killing her. It just wasn't safe for them to stay here too. If the killer tracked her somehow it would put Lin, and Tori, in danger. They might be risking too much just visiting, but they were being cautious. Careful. Taking back roads to get to Tori's and double-checking to make sure no one followed them.

"Come back for breakfast. Feed her."

Greer smiled and hugged Tori. She and Locke stepped out into the night. A little light broke through the clouds, but the storm had let up... until a larger one came in later.

"Good night for photos. Low-hanging clouds. Bits of scattered light. Windy but not damaging. We could get some great drops blowing from the leaves. You in?" he asked.

"You asking to keep company or to keep me safe?" Greer asked.

Good question. He was a mess of emotions. Being with Lin tonight only made things more confusing. The love he felt for her filled him so full, it would be too easy to let it spill out on to Greer. For once, he clamped down on his impulse to tell her that he simply missed them together—partnering. Working. Having fun. Because that might lead to something that wasn't real. Something that couldn't be.

"Safety," he finally muttered.

"Okay. I need to get into civilian clothing, then you can follow me to the station to return the patrol car." After running the errands, Greer rode with Locke.

"You gonna be all right going back in the woods?"

"Of course." She clambered out of the truck and followed him.

He watched as she retrieved a camera he'd purchased for her. She studied it then brought it to her eye and adjusted the lens like a pro. He ached for old times. Times that were gone like a vapor.

"You need an extra jacket or anything?" he asked.

"Nah. I'm good."

They entered the woods. "There's a little clearing about a quarter of a mile back. Sweet spot. Then we can hit a meadow."

"The Larkspurs own a big pasture and in spring the weeds grow tall and yellow. I took some pictures of Lin out there a few weekends ago. Be a great place and they won't mind." Greer snapped a few photos, readjusted her lens. "I bought some new filter software. It wasn't expensive, but I can write it off on my taxes so it's an investment. Unfortunately it was on my laptop with the other editing software."

He hated she didn't have enough to splurge or felt the need to justify extra spending. Now wasn't the time to bring up writing her a check. That would come across a little cheap—and not in the financial sense. *Hey, here's some cash. See ya next trip.*

"You know, Greer—"

She shrieked and grabbed her shoulder, then yelped again.

What in the world?

"Locke! I've been…hit!"

FIVE

Locke's adrenaline kicked in and he dove onto Greer, bringing her to the ground and shielding her. Sticking out of the tree was a knife. "How badly are you hurt?"

"I—I don't know. I think just a graze. Stings." Greer held out her hand. Blood. Locke needed to assess the damage, but someone was out there and using them as target practice. He tore the bottom of his T-shirt and wrapped his hand in it, then plucked the knife from the tree.

"He's close. Or he's remarkably good from a fair distance." Twenty feet maybe. "Stay low and let's go." He pocketed the knife encased in the T-shirt and covered Greer as they made a mad dash through the woods. Moving targets couldn't be as easy for their assailant. He hoped. Once they made it to the truck, he peeled from the lot. If Greer hadn't been wounded, Locke would have given chase, but he wasn't sure about the damage.

Greer shrugged out of her lightweight jacket and tucked her shirt over her shoulder. "It's a nick but I don't think I need stitches. Burns like all get-out, though." Her breathing was shallow and her cheeks were bleached. Locke reached over and covered her ice-cold hand with his. "I'm sorry." He'd promised to protect her and she'd been wounded. Proof he was a failure all over again.

"Nothing to be sorry for." She shuddered and touched her shoulder. "Can I see that knife?"

Locke slipped the wrapped weapon from his pocket and handed it to her. She opened up the T-shirt and stared at it. "Twelve-inch blade?"

"I think so." He'd gotten a pretty good look. Nylon-wrapped handle that blended with the blade. "It's a throwing knife, Greer. For impalement. Those are finger holes at the bottom to help with slinging. Someone knew exactly what they were doing. If it wasn't windy…"

She shuddered at his implication. He might not have missed. He'd come close. Too close.

"They have a wheel of death at the carnival. A knife impaler," Greer said.

"Have they interviewed him yet? Have you?"

"I haven't. We have over one hundred employees to work through and the deputies have been diligent. It frustrates me that I can't fully do my job, and after this stunt… I'll be fortunate if they even let me near evidence. I need to take this to the station. Enter it. All the protocol."

"We need to get that wound cleaned up."

"They have first-aid kits at the station. Unless you have to go."

"I have some time." He drove her to the sheriff's station—a small brick square with an equal sized and shaped parking lot. Less than ten patrol cars were in the lot. Some personal vehicles lined the street. "Do y'all even have the manpower to handle this case?" he asked. "I can make one call to my sister—or Wilder—and have either one of them out here and on it." Wilder, his cousin, owned a world-renowned private security company and his sister, who had once been in the military and the Secret Service, now worked for him. "He followed us from the house. Which means we have to be way more careful and take even more extreme measures, especially where Lin is concerned."

"I was just thinking the same thing." Greer rubbed her temples. "As far as calling in your sister, I think we can do our jobs, Locke. We aren't hillbillies."

"I didn't mean that. I'm only saying they have high-powered equipment and their computer analyst—Wheezer—is a force to be reckoned with, and so is my brother-in-law, Evan."

Greer winced and shook her head. "First off,

what do we need an analyst for? We have nothing to dig into."

"Not true. He can turn up stuff that background checks can't. He could probably find something on Flip Bomer. Tiny Tim." He laughed. "I can't even say that with a serious face."

Chuckling, Greer folded the knife back into the strip of T-shirt. "Thanks for thinking of this." She held up the encased evidence.

"I may not want to be a cop, but I can't deny I bleed blue and know a thing or two, minus watching the police dramas on TV." He clambered out of the truck and she paused. "I'm going in. I was a witness. They'll want a statement. Don't worry. I won't say anything smart to the boyfriend, but fair warning—he would be wise not to say something smart to me." It rankled that she was seeing someone—or in the early stages of it—but it shouldn't.

"Locke…" Greer heaved a sigh. "Just…come on."

He followed her inside the station and remained quiet as colleagues and friends saw to her needs, cleaned her up and asked questions. Only when he was asked questions did he speak. The boyfriend wasn't around. There was a small sliver of satisfaction in that. He followed her to her desk, which was butted up against another.

A lanky deputy with a smattering of freckles and unruly copper-colored hair approached. "Hey, Ben." Greer pointed to Locke and introduced him. "Deputy Garrison," she returned to Locke. "Any news? I'm basically barred from investigating."

"Which stinks." He glanced at Locke. "Greer is one of the best investigators."

Greer's cheeks reddened. "Thanks, Ben."

"I'm switching out with Adam tonight. Every thirty minutes," Ben said. "But I don't know how long it'll last. Overtime and all. But we both agreed, we're happy to do it on our own time."

Locke studied him, unsure if he was being friendly or if there might be a crush hidden in there. Greer had no idea how attractive she was inside and out. It was part of her unintentional charm.

Greer stood. "I appreciate that, but it's not necessary." She eyed Locke and the war raged in her eyes again. "Locke and I are…we go back a ways, and he's going to be staying at the house a few days. On my couch."

Locke tried not to roll his eyes.

"Whatcha in town for?" Deputy Garrison asked.

Locke told him and the next few minutes they discussed tornadoes. How many Locke had seen. Been in. Filmed. Photographed.

"That's cool. Is it like that movie? The one with the twister?"

"*Twister*?" Locke smothered a laugh. "Yes and no. In real life, that belt wouldn't have held Helen Hunt and Bill Paxton. They would have been goners long before they tied it. Once the roar sounds, the whirlwind eats up everything in its path faster than you can even begin to imagine."

Ben stared at him then shivered. "You ever scared it'll get you?"

More times than he could count. "I don't do this job as a death wish. I'm not one of those. I make sure to stay in the safe zones, and I know when I need to tuck tail and get out of Dodge." But sometimes he'd cut it close for the shot. "That's why I'm a part of this project. People need longer warning times. And scientists need to know which storms will cause a tornado to help improve that."

"What about you, Greer?" Deputy Garrison asked. "You ever chase a tornado?"

Greer peered up at Locke, a whirlwind in her eyes. "A time or two," she murmured.

Dozens.

"Not for you?" he asked.

"I guess not." She turned to leave. "Please keep me posted on the investigation."

"Will do." He shoved his hands in his pockets. "Drive-bys start at midnight," he called.

She waved a hand, acknowledging him, and pushed the door open. Smelled like rain. It was almost ten o'clock. "You hungry?"

"No, but I need to eat."

"Where to?"

Greer rubbed her injured shoulder and scowled. "The carnival."

Locke slowly glanced over and eyed her. "The carnival? You serious? You jonesin' for a turkey leg or something?"

"No. I want to talk to the knife thrower."

That didn't seem like a great idea. She wasn't even supposed to be working the case. And if that wasn't enough, if the killer was there and found a prime opportunity, he might attempt another attack. Put her on the wheel of death and spin her right round in a really bad way. "I don't know, Greer..."

"This guy tried to put a knife in me tonight. And Thursday night. I can't even stay in the same house as my child. No one took my badge from me, Locke. No one is going to take away my ability to do my job—to hunt my killer like he's been hunting me."

He paused at the stoplight and peered into her brown eyes. No nonsense in them. She wasn't going to back down and if he didn't go with her, she'd go alone. He knew it. "Okay, but here's the deal. I'm in this with you. A partner. Private security. So I get to ask questions. I get to probe, too."

"A glorified babysitter?"

"Glorified babysitter. Special nanny. Manny. I don't care what you call it. It is what it is. Or I'm taking you back to the house, barricading the door with my body and not letting you out until morning." He returned her stubborn attitude and doubled it with a high dose of don't-try-me.

With fire in her eyes, she lit him up, and for a few seconds he thought she might give him another go, but she finally sighed and agreed. "You can't impersonate a police officer."

"I know that's illegal."

"And I know you're impulsive and act before you speak eight times out of ten."

"You're not wrong." He chuckled and she laughed. Locke turned left instead of right at the only stoplight on the square. "What if we find him?"

"I'm going to shoot him between the eyes," she said, but he heard the teasing behind it. Greer would never pop a cap in someone willy-nilly. But eight times out of ten Locke might. Not really.

"You're not carrying, are you?" she asked. Guess they were having the same thoughts.

Locke pulled through the gate at the fair. Town volunteers taking money at the gates had already packed up. The Ferris wheel lights were off, signaling the carnival was closed. "It's in my truck. But Alabama honors Georgia's conceal-to-carry permits." He gave a wide grin. "I'm free to wear this bad boy in my concealed holster."

"Well, don't."

"Greer, I'm not going to shoot him. I mean I might. But not in cold blood. I'd tell him to start running first. Grace and all."

Greer snorted at his joking. "You sure about this?"

"Yes."

He cut the engine in the parking lot, and they trailed through the mud in their hiking boots. The air was nippy. Cloud covering hid the stars and moonlight projected nothing but nefarious shadows that stretched across the makeshift field parking. Locke scooted closer to Greer as they marched their way through the carnival.

Wet pavement. Muddy grass. Extension cords. The smell of childhood memories. They strode past the filthy rides and strips of games. Hanging stuffed animals looked cheap and unattainable. Passing the carousel, Octopus and Smashinator rides, they neared the tent that held the wheel of death. What sane person would allow someone to stake them to the wheel only to spin it and toss knives, hatchets and darts at them? Locke wasn't sure he trusted anyone that much. Not even his mama.

Greer hesitated outside the dingy, white tent. A gust of wind rattled the entrance—a plastic door flap. "We can skip this," Locke said.

"No. We can't."

And Greer stepped inside.

Greer choked back fear. She was putting up much more bravado than she felt, especially with every throb of the knife wound in her shoulder. If he'd gotten closer. If it had been lighter. If… if…if… She inhaled and scanned the tent. Two sections of chairs for spectators. One middle aisle. At the back of the tent was a huge wheel covered in nicks. "Hello?" Greer called. "Jenkins County Sheriff's Department."

A lithe woman wearing a turquoise sequined dress stepped out from behind a back area in the tent. She wore huge feathers in her hair and her eye makeup matched her dress in shine and color. But her eyes were dark and guarded. "Can I help you?" Her gaze shifted from Greer to Locke, lingering a little longer than curiosity should have allowed. Yeah, he was a sight to see. Greer's protective and slightly jealous reaction surprised her.

"I'm Deputy Montgomery and this is Mr. Gallagher." No reason she needed his first name. "I'm guessing you're the impaler's assistant?"

"I am."

"Don't let her fool you. She's a *dead* aim." A deep voice laced with one too many cigarettes sounded from behind and in walked a shockingly attractive man in his early thirties. Hair as black as Locke's. But instead of blue eyes he watched her closely with eyes as dark as coal. He had a gypsy appearance. Tall. Built. Johnny Depp, only broader.

"I'm Deputy—"

"Montgomery," he said with a Cheshire grin and stepped forward, extending his hand. "I heard." If he'd inquired about her name, had he inquired about her home address? Broken in twice and tried to kill her? He glanced at the assistant, who stood scowling. Maybe it was her turn to feel jealous.

"And you are?" Locke commanded.

"Marco Wise. But friends call me Marty." He didn't look like a Marty. He absolutely looked like a Marco. "Are you looking for me?"

"I am. Could we see your throwing knives, perhaps?" Greer asked, then tossed in a sunshiny smile. "Please."

Marty held her gaze. "Can I ask why?"

"Does it matter?"

One beat. Two. Another grin, as if he had the

best kept secret. "Star, would you bring my set of knives in for the lovely deputy." He didn't even bother to look at Star. Was that her real name? "Pardon me for being so bold, but you have the most exquisite eyes. Burnt sienna with flecks of amber. Framed in spun gold. You could be a fairy-tale maiden." He spoke like he was from another time. He was frightening and alluring at the same time. "I also paint," he added sheepishly.

"With knives?" she asked, ignoring the unnerving description he gave of her.

He tossed back his head and laughed. Marty wore a white pirate's shirt and silky black pants with black riding boots. Maybe he was a pirate. Had he tried to steal her life tonight? "No, but that's not a bad idea."

Star returned and slammed the leather box on a skinny table near the wheel of death. "Anything else?"

Marty cocked his head. "No, I don't think so."

She spun on her stilettos. Greer noticed part of her costume was unzipped, as if she had been taking it off when they'd arrived. Or putting it on? Didn't Marty say she was an accurate thrower? But she was here. And so was he. Meant nothing. Either one of them easily had time to return from the woods to the carnival while Greer and Locke were at the station.

"Have you been here all night?" Greer asked before she disappeared behind the curtain.

"Yes, why?" Star turned and eyed her warily.

"Have you, Mr. Wise?" Greer swung her gaze from Star to Marty and back again. Tension mounted.

"I have. I had a show at seven. And then I wandered the grounds. I love the weather before a storm. Don't you?" he asked.

Was he taunting her?

"Okay, open up the box and let us see." Locke finally stepped up, aggravation and irritation front and center in his voice. Marty only grinned and opened the leather case.

A set of twelve knives.

Identical to the one thrown at them. Greer's throat swelled and her stomach knotted. But all twelve were here. "This your only set?"

"No. But these are the ones I threw at Miss Star tonight. Tomorrow, hatchets. You should come and watch." He closed the case. "May I ask why you're so concerned with the knives?"

"Because someone tried to nail her with one, and they're identical to yours. So, I gotta ask. Did you try to land one of these into the deputy?" Locke stood about an inch above Marty, and the menace in his eyes was palpable.

Greer had wanted to keep the happenings tonight close to the vest, but Locke, in his impulsiveness...

Marty raised a thick eyebrow. "Might you have led with that, Deputy? You're welcome to accompany me to my trailer—"

"Nice try, pal. She's not going anywhere with you."

Marty raked his hand through his shaggy bangs. "I see."

"I kinda don't think you do," Locke sneered.

"All my blades are in my trailer except the set I used tonight. They're very common. Easy to purchase online."

Greer tamped down her temper. Letting Locke this close to the investigation was a mistake. "Did you know Flip Bomer well?" Turn tactics.

"Ah, Flip. Everyone knew Flip."

"What about Tiny Tim?"

"Yes."

"Were they friends?" Greer asked.

"No one was friends with Flip." He picked up a knife, balancing the tip on his index finger. "I'll tell you a secret, Maiden—"

"Deputy."

"Deputy. Tiny Tim was a drug dealer more than he was a carnival employee. His death would be more about drugs or drug money than anything else. Flip knew about those drugs along with everyone else, so if Flip was blackmailing Tiny—it wasn't about something he wasn't hiding too hard." He inched his eyebrow farther north. "However, if everyone knew about the drugs…why wouldn't someone do something about it?"

Interesting question. One he seemed to already know the answer to. "What would it have been about?" Greer watched him effortlessly keep the knife perfectly still on his index finger while he kept his eyes on her.

"Well, I suppose that would be an investigator's job. Which I'm not. I know beautiful women. And knives." Another grin that ripped across her like icy claws. He popped the knife in the air, caught it and slung it at the wheel, landing it in the bullseye. "Anything else, Deputy?"

"No." Greer looked at Locke. "Ready?"

"Definitely." He glared at Marty and protectively shielded Greer as they left the tent. "Okay, that guy was a freak show. Spun gold. Really?" He tugged at her hair. "Flaxen. Maidens' hair is always flaxen."

She slapped at his hand and laughed. "How about you and Mr. Wise leave my hair out of your discussions."

"I didn't like him," Locke said. "Hair comments. Eye comments aside. He's creepy."

"But handsome."

"What?" Locke's indignation sent her into a spasm of laughter.

"Well, he was. I can't decide if he's trying to charm me or kill me. He sort of fits the build. Both have beards and mustaches."

"I need a funnel cake." He pointed toward a stand. Two older women were inside cleaning up.

"It's closed."

"Charm, huh? Watch the master. I'm about to charm them out of two funnel cakes. Extra powdered sugar. Maybe even a lemonade. And at no charge."

Greer had no doubt Locke would return with everything he asked for. He had a silver tongue and a way with his eyes, mixed with a lopsided grin and that deep dimple in his right cheek. "I'll be over here waiting while you finagle dessert. And I expect you to share."

About five feet away, he turned. "He was not handsome or charming." He gave her a somber look and pointed toward her. "Clearly your taste has gone downhill since me, counting the deputy boyfriend—who might not like you ogling a suspect in *your* attempted murder case."

He swaggered to the funnel cake stand. Greer admired his humor, his charm. His good looks.

Marty might be handsome in an exotic way, but he held no candle to Locke's perfectly symmetrical face. Square chin. Dazzling eyes. She needed to quit ogling *him*. She might also need to come clean about Adam. It was easier to let Locke believe that Greer was seeing someone. Not that he'd try to charm her again. They had more history between them than a college world-history textbook.

Greer leaned against the popcorn machine, the smell making her stomach rumble. Truth was the instant she chose to hide Lin from Locke, she knew it had cut ties for good.

One of the women laughed. Locke had those funnel cakes in the bag. Good, she was hungry.

A skittery feeling raced across her skin as a leather-encased hand covered her mouth and nose, yanking her behind the machine and into the shadows. Something sharp pricked through her T-shirt and into her ribs. Knife! "Not a peep," he said in a gravelly, Batman-type voice.

Greer fought as he hauled her about three feet away, his knife digging into her ribs. He dragged her through the side door to the fun house as she kicked and worked to reach her gun, but the way he had her confined kept her from it.

He toyed with a strand of her hair. Nausea rose in her throat. He flung her to the floor of the empty fun house. Strobe lights messed with her vision and loud music with too much bass thumped in her chest. Mirrors lined the black-and-purple-walled building. She was completely disoriented.

He held the knife to her throat with one hand while his other hand pinned her arms by the wrists above her head. "You're dead," he growled.

With all her strength, she came up and head-butted him. He released his grip and she kicked his gut and sprung up, reaching for her gun. He rolled behind a mirror. All Greer saw was herself in dozens of mirrors, some of them distorting her appearance and shape.

Where had he gone? She had to find him. He couldn't escape again.

She glanced around. Was that footsteps? She couldn't tell. Suddenly, her insides grew hot, her adrenaline raced. Was she having a panic attack?

Moving down one row, she turned left into a dead end. A figure in the mirror had her flinching. It was only her reflection.

"Greer!"

Locke. She didn't want to holler back and give away her position. She backtracked, weaving up and down rows until she froze. Dead in her tracks.

The faceless figure stared back at her, all in

black. She couldn't make out a single feature, which sent a chill up her spine.

He raised a knife. Drew back.

Something toppled her to the ground as a knife missed her and struck the mirror, which rained down in broken pieces.

Locke was on top of her back. Covering her. Who was covering him?

"We have to get out of here. We're on his turf," Locke yelled over the deafening music.

But they were so far in she wasn't sure where out was. Was the killer still inside, biding time? Waiting to strike again? Fear clung to every nerve in Greer's body.

"Left," Locke instructed as they got up. He led her down another section of mirrors, their reflections sending her into fresh waves of fear. Two rights. One more left and she felt a draft.

They were almost out.

Almost free.

She turned back.

The assailant's reflection taunted her in a mirror.

But he disappeared as quickly as he appeared. Greer whipped past Locke. He was not going to taunt her. To get away with trying to kill her. Terrified as she was, she had to go back in, but Locke grabbed her forearm and yanked her into the damp air.

"Oh, no, you don't." He kept a firm grasp on her and led her safely away from the fun house. "He knows the layout of that structure. He's baiting you, Greer. Don't fall for it. I won't let you fall for it."

Greer knew he was right but it sickened her. There were three ways to exit this thing. Not enough of them to cover each entrance and it wasn't safe to cover an exit alone. Looked like this guy was once again going to get away with the havoc he was wreaking.

"What happened?" Locke asked. "One minute I was getting funnel cakes—which I did—but I tossed them when the next minute you disappeared. I barely caught sight of him dragging you into the fun house."

Greer explained what happened as they made their way to the truck. "He's getting away with this!"

"No, he's not. We just need to regroup." He opened the truck door for her then jumped in the driver's seat.

"Locke," she said as the reality set in. "You keep putting yourself in dangerous situations on my behalf. I don't ever want to put you in that position again. You didn't ask for this."

He tucked a strand of hair behind her ear. "Neither did you. We're in this together."

It had been so long since they'd been a "together" in anything. She'd missed that.

"For Lin's sake," he added.

For Lin. Right. Of course. As they drove back to her house, Greer thought about the stolen laptop and how destroyed her desk was. It was like the killer had concentrated on that area. Why? Did he think she might have taken an incriminating photo? She had been taking pictures all day Thursday before the carnival began.

"Locke, I'd like to go through the photos I took on Thursday. What if there's something in one of them that can be useful? I know I'm grasping at straws, but this guy isn't going to stop until he's silenced me. We're racing against time."

And she was desperate.

SIX

Locke loomed over Greer with his steaming cup of coffee as she sat at her desk in the corner of her living room and plugged the memory card from her camera into his laptop, since hers had been stolen. He didn't bother to mention there was probably nothing to find. She needed some kind of sense of accomplishment. Being tossed off the case officially and coming up with dead ends couldn't be an easy pill to swallow.

The coffee was doing nothing for him. Greer had almost lost her life in the fun house tonight. Not so much fun. "I want to call Jody."

"You don't need to call your sister in, Locke. We've been over this before." She clicked through the digital gallery of photos, studying each one meticulously.

"I think we should have her come out and take Lin back with her. What if this guy realizes we have a daughter and he—he takes her?"

"Then you'll use your very special set of skills to get her back?" Greer asked.

"This isn't funny! Stop paraphrasing Liam Neeson movie lines!"

"I'm sorry!" she hollered, her face pale and a slight tremor in her voice. "I can't think about it. It scares me too bad. I'm not sending my baby away with strangers—even ones I trust." She laid her head on her hands. "I'm so frightened. I want my daughter. I want my life back."

Locke set down the coffee and kneeled next to Greer. "I'm scared, too, if it makes you feel any better. For Lin's safety, and yours. But he's been in this house. He's probably seen all the photos on the wall and already knows we have a daughter. And while we're being super careful and taking extra measures by going the long way to Tori's to ensure we aren't followed…we aren't perfect."

She popped up her head and gazed into his eyes.

"Maybe we move Tori and Lin somewhere else. Or talk to the sheriff about extra protection on Tori's home. We'll figure it out. You and me," he whispered. "Okay?"

She only nodded and he refrained from wiping her damp cheeks. He was supposed to be angry with her. Furious even. But right now, in this moment, she was so vulnerable. Broken. Frightened. He had nothing but compassion to give, to offer. He could not give her anything else.

He'd have to put his feelings on hold, work through them on his own time. Set aside everything except his focus on protecting her, supporting her—getting them all through this. Locke's greatest weakness was his lack of focus. He was everywhere. All over the place. His RV was covered in yellow-and-blue Post-its, reminding himself of everything from being on time to picking up a loaf of bread.

But he was pretty sure he didn't need a Post-it to remind him a killer was coming. With a vengeance. With death on his mind. And he was laser-focused. Locke would just have to pull from whatever deep parts were in him and remind himself that his pain and his anger weren't the top priorities. Those feelings would end up getting them killed.

"Let's just look at the photos. We can talk about Lin and what's best for her in the morning, and instead of your boyfriend driving by every thirty minutes to keep an eye on you, ask him to drive by Tori's, then let's call and let her know." He rubbed his two-day-old scruff. "I'll keep you safe. And I'll trust him to keep my daughter safe." Not that he wanted another man protecting his daughter, but those were the kinds of feelings he was sacrificing himself on. He was swallowing pride. Falling on his sword. All the clichés that came with sacrifice. He'd do it for Lin. For Greer.

"I can do that much. I'm trying to keep it together, Locke. I really am. But I'm stretched thin, ya know?" Her lower lip trembled. This woman had come home to take care of her ailing mother, then dealt with a pregnancy alone—even if she didn't have to—and then all the responsibility of caring for two was dumped on her. Plus working three jobs. Then her mama died. Her dad was out of the picture.

Now a killer was after her. And Locke had shown up. Maybe…maybe he was supposed to be here now. Not just for the stormy season… but for Greer's stormy season. His mama would say, "God does mysterious things. Always right. Always perfect. Timing impeccable."

Locke wasn't so sure. He felt like the perfect timing to know about Lin was when Greer found out. But he was here. And Greer needed him. And maybe…maybe he needed to be needed. Maybe he could do something right and not fail. To remind him that there was more to the world than nature. Like people. Real living, breathing people. "Greer, you're the bravest and strongest woman I've ever met. If anyone can navigate this messed-up situation, it's you. If anyone can figure out who this guy is, it's you. If anyone can rise above the challenge, Greer—honey—it's you." He tucked that untamable lock of hair behind her ear again. "It's you."

Her eyes misted and she sniffed. "How can you say that? Are you…aren't you angry with me?"

"I'm a lot of things with you, Greer." A tempest of emotions swirled from the funnel in his heart. Love, laughter, hope, disappointment. Fear, fury. First kisses. Last kisses. All of it all thrown in, ravaging every part of him. It was the most confused he'd ever been. "But we have to set aside personal feelings and work through this first. Then we work through everything else." If he could. Could he? He stood, reached over her and clicked the mouse—the computer screen came to life.

Conversation over. He'd had all he could in the personal department for the time being. He clicked through shot after shot of the storm system coming in. Greer had talent. Always had. A few of Lin were mixed in and he chuckled. "She likes having her picture taken." It was like she was posing for each one.

"Well, she's had a camera thrust her in face since birth. She's used to it." Greer laughed, then cleared her throat.

Locke was leaning over her, using the mouse, her hair tickling his nose. His lips were close enough to steal a kiss on her ear or the tender area of her neck below her lobe. "You have another chair?" Time for Greer to take the helm and for Locke to sit next to her at a safe distance that didn't give him a heady feeling or tempt his impulsive side to do something that would be a huge mistake.

"Just bring one from the kitchen table."

He rushed into the kitchen and brought back a wooden, straight-back chair. "Okay, I'm ready."

"Cindy wanted pictures of the carnival, but I also took some personal photos in the mix. It's possible I got something that I wasn't meaning to." She paused, then pointed at the screen. "Hey, there's Marty!"

"Marty, the handsome possible killer."

Greer rolled her eyes. "Look, he's with his assistant and Tiny Tim. What do you make of it?"

Locke frowned. "The thing is, these people are coworkers. Even like family. So, what might be innocent, might be innocent. Or…it might not. All we know is that the knife wounds on Tiny Tim match the same knife wounds on Flip. There are several possibilities, but the one I'm leaning toward is Flip blackmailed the killer— for what, we don't know—and he killed him for it. Why he murdered Tim is another mystery. Marty seemed to let on like he knew. But he could also be toying with us."

Greer faced him and chewed on the tip of her thumb. "The question is what was Flip black-mailing him over? And who is the killer?"

"I think it might be easier to find out the *what* than the *who*. Rumors fly. People talk. If we can find out the *what* it could lead us to the *who*."

Smiling, Greer nudged Locke playfully. "You sure you didn't miss your calling?"

"I'm sure." Did she want him to be in law enforcement? Even now she was encouraging him. He'd always suspected that was part of the reason she'd broken things off. He wasn't the man she wanted him to be. It wouldn't be too far of a stretch. Had she realized—before finding out about Lin—that she didn't want to travel the world, photograph storms...be with Locke? He couldn't think about it. Didn't want to. "I'm going to nuke my coffee." Nurse his wounds. He walked to the kitchen.

"Locke, I think we need to find out how many men work the fun house. He was overly famil-iar with it."

Locke reentered the living room, glad to keep the conversation on the case. "I agree. Could you recognize his voice?"

"No. I don't know if he was masking it to pro-tect himself in case I knew his voice, or in case I'd recognize it later on if I interviewed him. I doubt he'd know I've been basically banned from working the case. Adam and Ben are over interviews. They're still working through the crowd from Southern Comfort that night to see if anyone can place Ray Don there during Flip's murder and my attack. No one seems to be missing a maintenance uniform. So he either has one or someone is lying."

Locke sipped his coffee. The last thing he needed was more caffeine. "Marty Wise fits the build of your attacker and he's a skilled knife thrower."

"There are always backups. Someone else who knows how to throw knives and knows the layout of the fun house. You really think it's Marty Wise?"

"I don't know. I know I don't like him. I know he's hiding something and that assistant, Star—she's shady. I don't trust him. I don't trust any of 'em."

"Neither do I." She yawned and clicked through more photos. An hour later, they still had nothing that looked suspicious. It was nearing early morning hours. "I have to get some sleep, Locke."

So did he. His eyes burned and he could hardly keep them open. "Wake me early to see Lin. I didn't realize how much free time I'd have when I took this job."

"You like having free time?"

"I like not having a schedule."

"Yeah," she whispered. "I know. 'Night."

Why did it feel like Greer had just closed a door in his face?

Saturday morning brought a nip in the air, but sunshine to the gray days that had been going on since last Thursday. They'd stopped by to see Lin first thing this morning—going the long way around and using country back roads to ensure they hadn't been followed, that it had been safe. After leaving Tori's, they ate breakfast at Pearl's café. Regulars had perched on stools at the counter. The stares hadn't been super pleasant, but Greer couldn't hide who Locke was anymore. Unfortunately, the questions his presence would raise when he wasn't around to hear would be painful. Were they getting back together? Where has he been? They would all look at him as if he was a deadbeat dad. But he'd been proving he was good with Lin, even if he seemed nervous around her. She'd even reached for him twice—after he'd fed her pancakes this morning at Tori's.

No one could say her baby girl wasn't smart. Reach for the man who would spoil you rotten. Locke had always spoiled Greer. He was a romantic at heart. He'd never admit it, but he was. Flowers for no reason. Dancing in the middle of the storm. Kissing on a carousel. They'd ignored the one at the fair, as if they didn't have a romantic history with the ride. Easier for them both.

Now, it wasn't quite noon and Greer stood staring at Mama's garage. Unable to investigate officially and not much else happening in town, she was fit to be tied and as antsy as Locke on a normal day. If the sheriff knew she'd been unofficially investigating, he'd give her the business, but she couldn't sit on her hands. Except here she was, doing just that. Sort of.

This chore was never-ending and it was nice to have some help.

Locke looked at a ten-speed bicycle. "This was yours?"

"Yes, and I don't see me riding it ever again so I'm adding it to the list." She'd been going through boxes and clutter for weeks, posting things on the online swap-and-shop sites. Making a little extra money. Every penny helped. She might get fifty bucks for the old red bike. Might not be much to someone, but it was diapers and baby food to Greer.

Two elementary-aged boys pedaled on the sidewalk across the street. "Hey, Miss Montgomery. You need us to rake gum balls? We're doing it for ten dollars!"

She needed someone to cut down the sweet

gum tree altogether but it was great shade. "Sorry, guys. I'm doing my own raking."

"Are you going to sell the house?" Locke asked.

"No, the payments are pretty low and it's all Lin and I need." Quiet street. Mostly older neighbors, but the yard was a nice size and the backyard was already fenced in, which made it safer for Lin to play out there when she got old enough. At some point it would need a new roof and the siding needed paint.

Locke left the bike and walked around the front yard, staring at the house. "You got a ladder?"

"Yeah." She walked out of the garage. "Why?"

"Gutters need cleaning out. I'm gonna do that."

He wanted to clean the gutters? For Lin? Lin wouldn't care if the gutters ran clear or were clogged until kingdom come. All she cared about were clean diapers, bottles and baby food. But their hands were tied in the investigation and they were both feeling it. Doing household chores would help them both work through the dread of uncertainty, and the fact that a killer was after Greer and Lin could even be in possible danger. "That's not necessary. I can do it or—"

"Don't even say *the deputy* will. I can do it. Where's the ladder?"

"Side of the house."

He stomped off to the ladder. When he returned, he leaned it against the siding near the downspout. "I need a trowel and a bucket." Jaw clenched, no eye contact. He was irritated. She sighed and dug around until she found what he needed, plus a pair of extra large gloves. Hollister must have done some yard work for Mama and left them. She handed them to Locke, who was standing at the foot of the ladder.

"He's not my boyfriend. We aren't dating. I'm not interested in him like that, and he's not interested in me. There. Now, you know."

Locke's eyes lightened and his jaw unclenched. "You sure about that?"

"Does it matter?"

He climbed the first rung. "I suppose not. It's just…nothing." He continued to climb. "Thanks for the gloves and trowel."

It was just what? Greer didn't bother to press. She wasn't sure she wanted to know. Returning to the garage, she sorted and listed things she could part with. Things Hollister wouldn't want. If she called him and told him what was going on, he'd be on the first flight out from Mississippi. If she didn't call him and he found out, he'd kill her himself. Former Navy SEAL big brothers were like that.

Groaning, she picked up her cell phone and called him.

"What's up, little sis?" The sound of a four-wheeler cranking filtered through the line.

"What are you doing, Hollis?" she asked.

"About to do some training. What are you doing?" Hollis was the director for the search-and-rescue. Had been for the last six years.

"Cleaning out Mama's garage."

"Put it off and I'll come next weekend and help you. You shouldn't have to do it alone, Greer. Please don't do it alone." Hollis had a gruff voice like their father, but he wasn't anything like Dad, even if he looked just like him, too.

Greer peeked out the open garage. Locke was humming and scooping gunk out of the gutters. "I'm not...alone."

"Adam there with you?"

She sighed. "No. Hollis, I have to tell you something. Two somethings and before you drop what you're doing and come with an arsenal of guns, hear me out. First, I'm fine. Really."

"Greer, you're doing a terrible job at keeping me from my arsenal of guns and flying out this very second. What's going on?"

"Locke is here. Cleaning out...my gutters."

Silence.

"That deadbeat jerk! You let him—"

"He didn't know about Lin. I never told him." And she'd never told Hollis. Only Mama. Mama, who had begged her to give Locke a chance. But Greer couldn't. And she wasn't sure what she was going to do now.

"He didn't know about… You kept it… Greer!"

"Well, he knows now."

"And he's cleaning out your gutters? What does that mean?"

Greer blew away a strand of hair sticking to her cheek. "It means my gutters were full and he's… I don't know. Working things out in his head." Locke had to stay busy to think. Never could rest. Be still. "But that's not why I called." Greer inhaled deeply and let everything that had happened since Thursday spill over the line. "I'm fine, though. Locke is staying here. At the house. Platonically. We're over and—"

"Greer Annabeth Montgomery! I am not concerned about where Locke is sleeping—at least not this second. I am worried about your life. I'll be on the next flight out."

"No! No." Greer breathed deep a few times. "Hollis, I get you want to come and protect me. I do. But we're doing everything we can, and Locke is here. He can clean gutters, and he can look out for me. You know he can. You know his family and how he's been trained."

Hollis grunted.

"Do you really think his dad, his grandpa—his cousin, whom you know well—will have let him slip through the cracks?"

"Wilder Flynn wouldn't let his cousin be defenseless."

No, he wouldn't. Greer stole another peek as she edged out of the garage. Locke's arms were defined, cut. His T-shirt stretched tight against a wide back that tapered at the waist. He probably still practiced his karate katas every morning and hung a punching bag from a heavy tree near his camper. Did crunches and push-ups before calling it a night. A zing hit her middle and she flushed, then beelined it back inside the garage. "If I think it's too much for us, for our department, I'll ask you to come. You know I will."

Hollister sighed. "I'll be praying. What's going to happen with you and him concerning Lin?"

"I don't know. He doesn't want kids."

"Well, he should have thought about that before—"

"I gotta go right now." She had stuff to do and didn't need a lecture from Hollis. Locke hadn't mentioned not wanting Lin since he'd found out about her. If anything, he seemed determined to have a role in her life. But for how long? "Love you."

"Love you. Be safe." He hung up and Greer wasn't a hundred-percent sure she wouldn't see his face in a few hours. She went inside for a drink and when she returned Locke was sitting on a patio chair in the garage, his hair damp around the temples, the edges curling. Like Lin's.

"Gutters are clear."

"Thank you. You want a drink?"

"I'm gonna wash my hands and get some water. That okay?"

"You know it is." She smiled.

A few moments later, Locke returned with a clean T-shirt, face and hands, and a bottle of water in one of them.

"I saw you on the phone."

"Hollis. I updated him."

Locke's right eyebrow inched toward his hairline. "How long until he arrives?"

"He says he won't." She shrugged.

"I need a change of scenery. I'm coming out of my skin."

Only a few hours and he needed a new view. He was proving her point that he couldn't settle down and be happy without even realizing it. A few Saturdays working on the house and in the yard would get old to Locke at some point and he'd fly the coop, devastating Lin. "What do you want to do?"

"Sky is overcast. I could get some great shots with light streaming through the trees, like a cascade. Put them up on my website gallery. Park is public. We can be careful."

Greer would love to sink into photography and leave the worry of a killer behind. But that would never happen. "I'll go if we're careful."

Twenty minutes later they pulled into a parking spot at Goldenville City Park. Locke unloaded the camera equipment from the trunk and Greer donned her camera.

A creepy feeling crawled across her skin.

"Greer? What's wrong?"

Like a gazelle's instinct when it knew a lion was lurking, Greer raised her head and scanned the park. A few other families were enjoying the brief minutes of nice weather, though the ground was muddy in spots. Dog walkers. Nothing perilous, but that nagging feeling wouldn't let up. They'd been super careful on the drive over. Hadn't noticed a tail on them. "I'm jittery is all." She had her personal weapon concealed. "Are you carrying?"

"Yes, why?"

"Good." Made her feel safer. She decided to try and shrug off the sensation of intrusive eyes watching, biding time. "You still like to sight-see when you have downtime?"

Locke shrugged and used his camera to take a few shots of the surroundings. "For the most part. That and take photos on my own time. Try new foods."

Freedom. He did what he wanted, when he wanted.

"Did you know there's this burger joint in Collierville, Tennessee, where they never ever change out the grease they cook their burgers and fries in? It's the best burger and fries you'll ever eat."

"Yeah, because you'll die before dessert."

Locke grinned, and she laughed. He captured it on film. "I ate there three times when we were in the Memphis area. Couldn't get enough. When Lin can eat burgers and fries and enjoy it, I'll take her."

Not *we*. *I*. "Locke, what exactly are your intentions with Lin?"

A divot formed along his brow. "What do you mean? I intend to be in her life. I'm her dad. I know I said I didn't want kids, but I have one now. Things have changed on a dime."

"But how?" A whole new fear swept over Greer. "Just gonna swing into town when you're in the area? Take her on a few long weekends? Show up at her graduation and maybe birthdays if you're able? Because I'd rather you not be around at all than be a revolving door she can't count on to be there when she needs you."

Lowering his camera, he cast a long glance at Greer. "You think I wouldn't be here if she needs me, don't you?"

"Tornadoes come first to you, Locke. They don't wait for when it's convenient for you to photograph. Lin might be top priority now and maybe even two or three years from now, but at some point, she will become less and less of one. Until she's not one at all. And that's not fair to her."

"Is that so?" he murmured and his gaze reflected the wound Greer had inflicted. She held her ground, clung to the truth. A truth she'd experienced firsthand.

"It is."

He pinched the bridge of his nose, squeezed his eyes closed. "Why did you ever tell me you loved me?"

"What?" When? What did this have to do with anything?

"You once told me you loved me. You'd go anywhere with me. We talked about marriage… a lifetime together…"

"And that never came to be. Did it? We were together over four years. I never saw a ring."

"Because I bought it right before you left to

take care of your mama. I planned to propose when you came back. But you broke things off. So, yeah. You never saw a ring."

And she never would now. Locke was going to propose. But after a week of being home, she'd discovered she was pregnant with Lin. While she was choosing to end things, Locke had been deciding to make them last forever.

"And before you say anything, it had nothing to do with what happened before you left. It wasn't a ring out of guilt for crossing lines. It wasn't a ploy to make those crossed lines official so they could keep happening. It was simple. I loved you. I wanted to be with you. Always."

Past tense. All past tense. Greer could hardly stay on two feet. Even if he had proposed, it wouldn't have turned out well because Greer had gotten pregnant.

"I don't know what to say."

"Well, it won't be *yes* anymore, now will it?" He tossed his hands in the air. "And I'm glad. Because you obviously never loved me. Love thinks the best about the other. You clearly think I'd be the worst father ever to walk the face of the earth." He froze, eyes wide, as if a sudden reality hit him. "I was setting myself up for rejection the whole time, wasn't I? You would have never married me."

Locke stormed off to the seesaws, pain etching his face. Pain etched her heart.

What he'd said wasn't true. Greer had loved Locke with everything in her and she always thought the best of him, but when it came to fatherhood… Well, she wasn't sure anymore what she believed.

She waited around until he returned. His face was a mask. She had no idea what he was thinking and she was too emotionally exhausted to get back into it. "I got what I needed. No sense staying out here any longer than necessary."

Locke stayed nowhere any longer than necessary.

SEVEN

Locke noticed Greer bouncing her leg as she sat in the passenger seat in his truck. After returning from the seesaws it had been beyond tense. It was one thing for Locke to be aware he'd screw up being a dad. It was a whole other sinking feeling to know that the woman he'd loved like crazy thought it, too. Enough that she'd hid the child from him. He had to push it aside for now. Locke and Greer had to get along and be able to be in the same room without fighting or tears. Focusing on the case was their only safe line of communication.

"You're going nuts not being active on this investigation, aren't you?"

"Completely. The carnival is in full swing right now. He's there. I'm here." She pulled out her phone. "I gotta do something."

"Who are you calling?"

"Adam. He's on duty today. Hey, Adam," she said. "I need an update… I will. No, I'm on camera duty tonight. Community dance. I doubt I'll be doing any dancing, but yeah. I'll save you one if I have time."

Locke balled a fist tighter than the one in his gut. He had to get over this. He didn't even love Greer. They were over. Done. Dunzo. They were free to dance with anyone they wanted. Locke rolled his hand in a fast, circular motion, letting Greer know he was ready for her to wrap it up.

She scowled. "I'll talk to you later." She ended the call and made a display of putting away her phone.

"Well?" he asked.

"He's at the carnival now. Doing some follow-up with the employees. No one is being overly cooperative. Not even Rudy and Jenna Dennsion."

"The owner-managers? Why wouldn't they want a killer caught?"

"Maybe there's more hidden than we know. Secrets seem to run deep in that place."

Tension mounted. Secrets ran deep in all sorts of places. "What is this about you taking photos tonight? You know a storm's coming in, right? In fact, all of lower Alabama is in for some serious weather. Flooding. Tornadoes. It's going to get bad for everyone."

"Well, for us, it won't get bad until after ten," she said.

"Could be earlier. Later."

"Part-time job. Every spring the Parks and Rec department hosts a community dance. Live local music. Kicks off the BBQ fest, so it'll be smelling like something out-of-this-world. The actual contest and judging is tomorrow afternoon."

Back at her place, she sat down with Locke's laptop. Going through photos seemed to make her feel better. Locke snagged a cookie from the jar.

"When will you be swinging through again?" she asked.

"I don't know." He'd make a way somehow. Storms didn't sit down and make a plan along with Locke's. They just happened. "After June I have a good bit of time off. You know this about tornadoes. I can come back then. Stay for a few months. Or take Lin to see my mama. My sister."

Greer bristled.

"Greer, I'm not asking to take her into a tempest. And I can't deny I have a daughter. I can't just pretend she doesn't exist or that I don't want her. You didn't want kids and then she was here and you did. I guess it's the same."

"No, it's not. The truth is I always wanted children. Why do you think I brought it up that one time? The one time it turned into an argument. I let it go and agreed. Pretended I didn't really want them either because I... I didn't want to lose you. You said I never loved you. Wrong. I did. So much I was willing to give up dreams of children to be with you."

Locke raked his hands through his hair. "But why hide her?"

"I told you why. You had dreams and I didn't—"

"Want me to give them up. I'm not buying that."

"It's true. And I knew you wanted to have a life where you could come and go as you pleased. That's not the kind of dad Lin needs."

"We're going to have figure something out then. Now that I know... I can't pretend I don't."

Greer rubbed her temples. "I know. Have you told your mama yet?"

"I haven't told anyone, Greer. I'm still processing it myself." He carried his coffee cup to the kitchen and washed it out, put it in the drying rack. "I'm going to the photo shoot with you tonight. Until I have to leave for my job, and I'm happy to help you with the shots because I'd like you to come with me when it's time for me to head out."

"Storm chasing?"

"Yes. You don't need to be alone."

"I don't have to be alone."

No. But he'd feel better if she were with him

even if they were like oil and water right now. "It'll be fun." He hoped.

"I'll think about it." She checked the time on the microwave. "We need to get Lin to the Woolridges' soon. I'll pack her bags, then we can swing by Tori's and pick her up. Drop her off on the way to the dance. It's on the fairgrounds."

Locke would feel better having Lin at the Woolridges'—with a man in the house. But he sure wouldn't be telling Greer that. It might unleash a women's equality war, and he had no doubt that Greer could keep Lin safe. But having that added measure of protection made him feel better. It was what it was.

And if they were going back to the carnival site, Locke would make sure he was carrying.

Greer checked her cell phone. Almost seven. After Lin's afternoon nap, they spent an hour or so playing with her, then they ran to the café to eat dinner. The people at the diner had been more cordial than the quizzical looks given to them the last time they ate together had implied. It wasn't really fair to Locke to assume he was the bad guy, leaving Greer to do everything alone. She felt guilty for that. She'd prayed and fretted—more fretting than praying—and made the choice. That was that. No going back, but that didn't assuage the guilt. Locke may one day leave them if she let him back into their lives, but he'd been sticking *this* whole thing out with Greer. Been by her side, helped with Lin, risked his life on more than one occasion and that meant something to her. Meant more than it should. If only Mama was here to shed some light on the situation. She'd urged Greer to let Locke know about Lin. Even if she were here to give advice, Greer was a pro at not taking it.

Greer and Locke had dropped off Lin at the Woolridges' with the assurance Lin would be fine, but Greer would worry, anyway. Seemed like worry was a moth, and Greer was the flame. And her poor stomach was a sweater. Eaten up with it. And while she tried not to—and even repeated scriptures about not fretting and trusting God—she was still worried and fearful. God had her in the palm of His hand. He could be trusted to work everything out for good. She knew that in her head.

How did she make a scripture become real in her heart?

Now, Greer parked at the carnival. "The pavilion is on the east side of the grounds near the BBQ tents. I'm going to be hungry all night."

Locke chuckled and retrieved his camera equipment. "We need tripods?"

"No."

"I'm grabbing both sets of lenses, just in case."

"Okay," she mumbled. Everyone was out tonight, dancing and laughing, and she was capturing their fun memories while trying to keep her own terror at bay on the inside. It was hard to talk lenses and tripods when a murderer was roaming around ready to steal, kill and destroy her. She slipped her camera around her neck and pocketed a fresh memory card. "The idea is family fun, and if we get a few couples in love, hey, all the better." For them.

"Roger that." Locke closed the trunk and adjusted his black jacket. He'd slipped his gun inside, no doubt. They trudged through the muddy grounds, the smell of cooking pork and spices wafting in the cool evening air. The clouds moved as if racing to get to the next place. She was sick of a pasty sky.

Clear lights twinkled from the pavilion rafters. At the far end, a local band played light country rock. Greer captured the lights. The romance. The band.

Locke ventured outside the pavilion, catching the stormy skies as a backdrop to the soft lighting inside. Locke always had an amazing eye. An incredible gift. Greer loved photography and was good at it. Good enough to make some extra income. But Locke was in a league of his own. His photos were pure art.

"Hey, hey," Adam said with a grin. No longer

in his deputy's uniform, he was dressed in relaxed jeans and a 'Bama sweatshirt, but he still wore his radio. Unofficially on duty. "How's the photo shoot going?"

Greer snapped a photo of him and grinned. "It's going. Any news from earlier?"

"You'll be interested to know that two games, three rides and one partial event were closed during the time frame right before and during your attack in the woods. I've secured alibis for four out of six." He folded his arms over his chest and watched as folks line-danced. "Jewel was missing. A Bolt Masterson shut down his game. And while Marty Wise was seen around, his event was closed, and I have no alibi for Star Jumper. We've been getting a count on how many employees work or have worked in the fun house. About eight so far. Marty Wise and Bolt Masterson are in that group, which puts them at the top of my list. We questioned them, but they have alibis for that night."

"First of all. Jumper? Is that really Star's last name?"

Adam chuckled. "Hippie parents?"

"I guess. Secondly, these people are keeping secrets and I wouldn't put it past them to cover for one another. I don't trust their word."

"I don't either. We'll keep digging, though." The band switched gears and slowed the music.

Couples left their lines for pairs. "You wanna dance?" he asked.

Did she? She glanced across the pavilion. Locke was engaged in a conversation with an older man and pointing to the lighting and his camera. The man never met a stranger. Did she want to dance? Yes.

But not with Adam.

Her heart crunched against her ribs, the ache so sharp she needed to sit down. "I'm on duty. Photo duty, that is."

"Or maybe I'm not the right dance partner." His gaze followed hers to Locke. Locke turned, made eye contact with Greer. Held on.

"It's complicated," she murmured and forced herself to look away. "I'm sorry."

Adam nodded. "He'll be gone in a few days, Greer. That doesn't seem too complicated. And...it was just a dance, not a marriage proposal." He grinned, then sobered. "Be careful tonight."

She was well aware there was more in the air than romance. There were other things...like homicide.

When Adam was long gone, Locke returned. He stared at her, his eyebrows asking all sorts of questions. But he'd get the same answer as before if it was about Adam. The lead singer belted out a ballad in his tenor voice. It was a song she and Locke both loved.

"You want to dance?"

Yes. "I don't think so."

"One dance, Greer." He didn't wait for her to protest. He grabbed her hand, twirled her in a circle and led her onto the dance floor. Their cameras clunked against one another. Locke paused and slid his camera around, so it now hung down his back instead of his chest. "That's better." He drew her to him. Frowned. Swung her camera to her back in the same way, then held her in a close embrace. "No...that's better."

Briefly, she felt safe. Like other couples here, they were simply enjoying the company and the night. No one wanted her dead. Her daughter was equally safe. She wasn't alone in life and raising Lin. She lost herself in the daydream, settled into the rhythm as Locke masterfully led them to the song. Swaying. He hummed to the tune, the vibrations tickling her scalp where he rested his chin. His subtle cologne toying with her senses. His warm hand enveloping hers, holding it to his chest.

The song came to an end and so did this charade. She peered into his eyes. He brushed a strand of hair from her face, his fingers lightly skimming her forehead, temple and ear, then lingered in her hair before trailing feather-soft down the side of her neck. "I'm so mad at you, Greer," he murmured.

Tears stung the back of her eyes along with a heavy dose of confusion.

"So, how is it you still make my heart race like crazy? How is it I can be so hurt and rejected and still want nothing more than to kiss you right here, right now? I want to forget there's a storm coming. I want to ignore every single person looking on and just have this moment."

She could barely swallow; her throat had turned to dust. He framed her face, and she didn't have the fight to say no. To break away. To remind him of all the reasons this was so wrong. Because she wanted the exact same things. She hadn't meant to hurt him. Hadn't even crossed her mind he would feel rejected. She honestly believed being released from his parental duties would be a breath of relief. She was giving him the out he'd eventually want, anyway.

And how could she be so afraid of the pain, which would soon be coming now that he'd re-entered her life, so afraid of him leaving her and Lin and want him to kiss her more than anything in the world, too? To keep holding her. Keep making her feel secure. Beautiful.

His eyes remained on hers, darting back and forth and searching. His nostrils flared and his jaw worked. Then he leaned in and bypassed her lips, placing a gentle kiss on her brow. "But I'm not going to."

When had Locklin Shane Gallagher ever had an ounce of restraint?

Or was he angry and hurt more than he was tempted?

"I'm going to the restrooms," she croaked. Tearing from the pavilion dance floor, she raced through couples who were indulging in a kiss or two. She darted toward the portable bathrooms. Normally, she'd turn up her nose, but right now she'd take any escape from what she was feeling. From the confusion waging war in her heart.

As she rounded the shadowy corner, her camera—still bobbing along her back—got caught. She turned as the man dressed in black used it to smack her face. The splitting pain seared up the side of her cheek, dazing her.

He put her in a headlock and thrust her into the tiny portable bathroom.

Pitch-black inside and her head screaming in pain, she used instinct to fight. Her adrenaline sprinted through her veins as fast as fear pumped her heart. Slamming her against the side wall, he wrapped his gloved hands around her throat and squeezed. They were large hands. Strong.

The bathroom rocked as she struggled for freedom.

Greer couldn't breathe. It was like being inside

a stale and pungent coffin. Her lungs and throat burned like a wildfire. He pinned her against the wall, one hand around her throat. With the other, he brought out a knife. He bared his teeth in a sinister grin.

Raising the knife to the side of her cheek, he ordered in an eerie tone, "Shh-hh…"

Panic flooded her and vomit reached her throat as he pressed the cool metal to her cheek, then she felt a small sting.

She fumbled for her camera. He'd used it against her, so she could turn the tables. She wasn't able to bring it up high enough to strike him, though.

But…she found the flash button. Switched it on. Closed her eyes.

Pressed the button.

The small bathroom lit up like the Fourth of July, blinding and stunning him. She used the sliver of opportunity, shoved him aside and busted through the door, gulping in precious oxygen. He bounded out behind her, and she drew her weapon.

Four teenage girls sauntered up, laughing. Not a care in the world.

The killer grabbed the brunette in the middle and snaked his arm around her neck. The girl's scream was cut off. Greer couldn't shoot. The creep pulled her several feet away, then shoved her toward Greer and the other girls and raced into the crowd. No one seemed to notice or care.

Greer gave chase, weaving through a maze of people. Carnival music blared and grated on her nerves like nails on a chalkboard. She caught a flash near the Ferris wheel and hauled off after him. But when she arrived, he was gone.

Vanished like the wind.

She found her cell phone and called it in. In a few minutes, Ben Garrison was on the scene. "Greer, I came as fast as I could."

The events replayed in her head and terror struck fresh. She bent over at the waist to breathe. "Girls. Find those girls. Question them."

"Already called Adam. He's on it. Greer, do you need a medic? You're bleeding a little and you have some bruising on your face. Did he punch you?" Ben asked.

"Greer!" Locke raced to her. "What Porta Potty did you use? The one in Timbuktu?" Suddenly he had her standing upright, his hands gripping her shoulders, fear in his eyes. "What happened?"

"I was attacked near the bathrooms. He dragged…he dragged me inside."

He grazed her face with his index finger. "What did he do?"

"Hit me with the camera." She gave Locke and Ben a play-by-play, then scanned the area.

Locke cocooned her with a grip that said no one was getting through it. She'd never felt more protected.

"I have all deputies on a search for him, Greer. They have copies of the sketch and will be asking around. Someone will have seen him. What was he wearing again? Just to be certain."

"Jeans. Hoodie. Ski mask. The girls won't have much more description than I gave, and I don't know how easy it will be to round them up. They took off running and I didn't recognize any of them." She exhaled heavily. "I need to help search."

"You need to get some ice on that face, and you know what the sheriff said. Let us work it. I'm heading back to the campers. If he's in one I'll find him. I promise." Ben patted her shoulder and jogged away.

"He's right, Greer. You need to ice that bruise and you have a cut." He opened and closed his fist. "Come on, I'll get you home, then we can regroup." Locke drew his weapon. "Just to be safe out here." He tucked an arm around her shoulder and led her to the parking lot.

Greer was pretty sure she wasn't going to be safe anywhere and that Ben wouldn't find this guy. He was like the wind. Here one second, gone the next. If they didn't get a lead soon, Greer feared she'd end up like the wind, too—gone. Permanently.

EIGHT

The smell of coffee permeated Greer's home. Outside the wind had picked up and rattled the windows. Greer and Locke had returned only twenty minutes ago. Greer had called Cindy on the way home and checked on Lin. She said they were doing fine. Lin was asleep and the boys had enjoyed helping babysit—they were even less rowdy, which was always a blessing.

After hanging up, Greer went back to searching photos. It was pointless, but Greer needed to feel like she was doing something productive to help. And this kept her occupied.

Locke entered the living room. "Turn on the news, Greer. There's been a terrible tornado sweep through Birmingham. I just got an alert on my phone."

Greer turned on the TV and they watched the massive destruction. "They'll be cleaning that up for months. God, help them," she prayed.

Locke set her cup of coffee on her desk, then

sat in the straight-back chair they'd left there, when they'd gone down this road before. "This is why we are doing what we do."

He was going into bad weather tonight. The thought made her nervous. But he was smart and careful. Didn't mean accidents couldn't happen. She prayed for him, too, and for a lead on this case.

He looked away from the TV and to Greer. "Anything?"

"No."

He checked his cell phone and frowned. "I don't have a lot of time. Storms are blowing into Rolling Hills in about two hours. I'll have to hit the road in a bit to get there."

Rolling Hills was outside of Jenkins County, about thirty minutes away. Locke said his tracking software and satellites had shown severe weather activity and a storm that could potentially produce a tornado. Not as bad as Birmingham. An F1, maybe F2. "I'll be okay—"

"I'd still like you to go with me, Greer. I can't—I won't leave you here alone. Not with a homicidal maniac out there. Not going to happen."

Truth be told, Greer didn't want to be alone. She was strong, trained and capable but that didn't mean she wasn't frightened or was too naive or prideful to admit she needed some backup. She felt the small cut the killer had left on her cheek and held back tears.

She wasn't weak and helpless.

"Let's just go through these photos." She plugged her memory card into Locke's laptop and backed it up to the early afternoon the day before the carnival actually began. She recognized some of the carnies in the background. She'd planned to blur them or crop them out. Now, with her editing software gone, she wasn't even going to be able to use them.

"Hey, that's Flip." Locke pointed at the screen.

"I know. We saw this photo the other night. He's standing at the funnel-cake booth."

Locke snagged a Post-it note and scribbled down the time stamp from the photo. "If we find more we can track him with the time stamps."

Locke may not have wanted to pursue a career in law enforcement, but he had the skills and eye for it. Greer clicked the mouse. One photo after another appeared onscreen. Jenna Dennison, the owner and manager. None with her husband, Rudy, in them. Star Jumper, the knife-throwing assistant, walking by the fun house. Nothing that raised a red flag.

She growled and rubbed her temples. "No one seems shady." She clicked again. "Who are these people hiding? Do you think they are, Locke? Hiding the killer since he's indirectly done so many of them carrying secrets a favor?" She clicked again.

"I don't know. Wait. Back up."

She clicked back.

"Can you zoom in on that one?"

"The campers?"

"Yes. The one behind the one in focus." Locke leaned forward. "I think I see something. Someone."

Greer clicked on the zoom tab. "It's a little grainy, but you're right. You saw a man."

Who was he?

"Do you still have the layout of campers? The one y'all used to identify who was staying where?"

"Yeah. Hold on." She stood and hurried into the kitchen and grabbed her bag, retrieving a manila file folder. She pulled out the map and handed it to Locke. He'd been messing with the grainy feed using his own photo software. Finally, he brought the man into better focus. "I'm not sure I recognize him."

Locke brought the photo back to its normal size. "Over there is Jewel's camper. It's blue and white. Stands out. So, this one…" He ran his finger along the map where Jewel's camper was and angled it some, held it up next to the photo and gaped. "That's Flip Bomer's RV, Greer! And the time stamp is only five minutes after the photo we found of Flip near the funnel cakes."

"Whoever is going inside might have known that Flip wasn't there. The door is open." Jewel had mentioned that Flip's RV had been rifled through before by someone looking for blackmail evidence. If this man knew Flip wasn't around, he might have been going inside to hunt for the information. Evidence. Greer jumped up. "We need to go back to the carnival right now. Let's find the managers and have them give us a name of this man so we can talk to him. I don't recognize him from any of the police interviews. This could be our break if he knows something…or if we discover he's the killer. He could have lifted a maintenance uniform easily enough." Excitement mixed with dread and fear of facing her possible attacker, but they might be one step closer and she was ready to have this behind her. Get her life back. Get Lin back.

Locke checked his watch. "If we hurry, I have time."

Greer printed the photo, grabbed a raincoat and slipped on her rain boots. Locke drove them to the carnival grounds and they made their way straight to Rudy and Jenna Dennison's RV. Greer knocked on the door. Rudy opened it.

"Deputy Montgomery, how can we help you?" Rudy glanced at Locke.

Greer held up the photo and Jenna peeked over Rudy's shoulder. "Can you tell me this man's name?"

"Well, sure," Rudy said. "Bolt Masterson. He works games."

Same guy who'd shut down his game when Greer had been attacked in the woods. "Can I ask why you're interested in him?" Jenna Dennison slipped under her husband's arm and ran her bottom lip between her teeth. "I mean…do you think he's involved in Flip's death?" She blinked several times and nervously glanced at Rudy.

Greer studied her. She wasn't doing a good enough job pretending to be nonchalant about her questions. "Do you think he could be?"

"Bolt?" She laughed, but too high-pitched. "I don't see how. Do—do you, Rudy?"

Rudy frowned. "I don't know. He's a quiet guy. Does his job. Keeps to himself most of the time. His RV is on the back south end. Can't say if he's there or not."

"What about you?" Locke asked Jenna. "Do you think Flip Bomer had any dirt on Bolt Masterson?" He cocked his head, squinted. He must be getting the same vibe as Greer. Jenna didn't like them probing about Bolt.

"If he did I wouldn't know what it was!" She clutched her chest as her face turned three shades of crimson.

"That's not what I asked," Locke said. "I asked if you thought he had any dirt."

Rudy slowly examined his wife and his brow creased.

She wouldn't look at him. Wouldn't look at Locke or Greer. "I have no idea."

Greer was certain she was lying. "Well, if you think of anything, let us know." Greer nodded her chin, and she and Locke headed toward Bolt's RV. "What do you think?" she asked Locke.

"That Jenna Dennison and Bolt Masterson have a secret of some kind. I'm not willing to make a judgment on what it is yet. And if our hunch is right, Flip may have known it, too, and blackmailed one or both of them. Bolt may have been at the camper trying to confiscate the incriminating evidence. Do I think he murdered Flip and attacked you? I can't say. But he had his game shut down during the attack in the woods. It's possible."

They weaved through carnies sitting under RV awnings imbibing liquor, laughing and listening to music. Cigarette smoke and stale festival food drenched the chilly air. "You know he won't admit anything including whether he found anything incriminating in Flip's camper. Not to mention, we still don't know why Tiny

Tim died—and before you get cheeky, you know who I mean. Don't be bringing Scrooge into it."

Locke chuckled as they approached Bolt's camper, then he knocked. "Seems pretty quiet inside. Maybe he doesn't keep to himself as much as they said." He banged on the flimsy door, then checked his watch. "Time is running out."

"Hey," a baritone voice boomed.

Greer turned as an ogre of a man stomped toward them. Military haircut. His body was close to the same as the killer's, but he had a smooth face. *Hmm.* "I'm Deputy Montgomery and this is my colleague. We're investigating the murders of Flip Bomer and Tim Maynard."

"I didn't do it." He frowned and paused in front of them.

"Maybe not," Greer said and retrieved the printed photo. "But you were in Flip's camper the day he died." She left out that they didn't actually have photos of him inside the camper or that Flip wasn't inside, too. Just Bolt opening the door. What he didn't know wouldn't hurt *them.*

Bolt's eyes hardened. "It's not a crime to stop by and see someone."

"No, I guess not. Except Flip wasn't home. He was at the funnel-cake stand. We have time stamps on the photos."

Cursing under his breath, Bolt shifted his

weight from one foot to the other and rubbed the back of his meaty neck. "I left something. No biggie."

"Left something?" Greer asked. Locke gave a slight shake of his head. He wasn't buying it, either. "Like evidence of a secret with Jenna Dennison?" She tossed it out, hoping for a reaction. If their guess was right, he might show some sign to confirm it.

Bolt's tough-guy exterior wilted like spinach in a hot skillet. "How'd you know? She tell you?"

Boom! "No. But is that what you were after? Photos of you and Jenna together?" Greer asked.

"No. Jenna and I haven't been a couple in decades. But Rudy wouldn't have let her hire me knowing we'd been married as kids."

Well, that wasn't the secret she was expecting. "You and Jenna were married?"

"For three years. She was eighteen. I was twenty-one. Things didn't work out. Then about five years ago I needed a job and I came begging. She hired me." He kicked a pair of muddy work boots out of the way.

"How did Flip find out?"

Bolt rubbed his brow. Could this guy be the same one who had attacked Greer? If so, he was putting on a pretty good performance. And again, he didn't match the physical description perfectly. But no one was matching one-hundred-percent. Could the killer have been disguising himself that first night, so employees wouldn't recognize him, besides possibly wearing a maintenance uniform as a disguise? Something to think about. If it was true, then any one of these people were suspects.

"He overheard us talking one night. Recorded it on his phone. Said if I didn't pay him ten percent of my paycheck, he'd play it for Rudy, who would fire me."

"Without the actual proof, Jenna couldn't risk firing Flip," Locke said. "He'd send it to Rudy, and he would fire you…but Jenna is the owner. She gets the final say. And if nothing is going on between you—"

"It isn't!" Bolt insisted. "Not that Jenna loves Rudy but…"

"But what?"

Greer connected the dots. "What does Rudy have on Jenna that keeps her from leaving him or firing him?" Rudy had been having an affair with Jewel at one time, so clearly his marriage with Jenna wasn't good. Jenna might not know about Rudy's affair since Jewel and Rudy were paying off Flip, but that didn't mean she didn't suspect he was having one. But she couldn't do anything because she had a secret of her own.

Bolt.

And something else. Whatever Rudy had on

her. She'd fill in Locke on what she knew about Rudy and Jewel later.

"Jenna's son. He...he isn't squeaky clean."

"As in?" Greer asked.

Bolt sighed. "Jenna's going to kill me." He ran a hand through his cropped hair. "Rudy knows that her son, Chris, supplies Tiny Tim with his drugs when we go through Birmingham. It's how he deals in the small towns. If Jenna leaves Rudy, he calls the cops and Chris goes to prison. If Jenna fired Flip, then Flip would rat out Chris or play the recording for Rudy and I'd get fired. She's stuck."

"You're not Chris's dad, though. Neither is Rudy. You said Jenna's son. Who's his father?" Greer asked.

"I don't know. She was sixteen when she had him. I didn't know her then."

Jenna had the greatest motive to kill Flip, but a man had stabbed him and then came after Greer. She shuddered. Could a man—maybe even Bolt—have done the job for her? She might have picked up Flip's tricks of the trade and blackmailed someone into doing it. But who?

They left Bolt's camper and walked in the chilly night.

"Do you believe Bolt Masterson? That he didn't find Flip's phone that day inside the camper?" Locke asked and paused to observe the sky. Black and gray with hues of purple. The rustling trees had quieted. The air was damp. They might not have to go to a neighboring town. Storms might be shifting direction. All the signs were there. Any minute Locke would say so.

"Yeah," Greer said. "Most people take their phones everywhere. But maybe he was looking for something else. Maybe he was hunting for information and photos that might incriminate Jenna's son. If she could get those, then she could have fired Flip."

"Except Flip would only have to call Birmingham PD and tip them off. They'd surveil Chris and catch him dead to rights at some point. The only way to keep Flip quiet was to kill him."

"Excellent point." Greer fell into step with him. "I want a crack at that camper. How much time do you have left?"

Not enough to be nosing through a camper, but Greer wouldn't back down. "Maybe ten or fifteen minutes." He turned from the parking lot back to the campers. "But don't you think something would have turned up when y'all searched it before?"

"Not if it's hidden well."

"Maybe it's not hidden there at all. Maybe he gets a locker or something in each town."

"Seems like a lot of trouble. And what about

when they hunker down in between? No, if he really has evidence, it's hidden all kinds of good." Greer picked up her pace as they approached Flip's side of the campers.

"I think Jenna Dennison had a lot of reasons to kill Flip and Tim Maynard."

Greer agreed. Both of them could get her son thrown in prison. "Let's do a quick sweep."

They slipped under the yellow crime scene tape. Greer opened the door. "And pray for a break."

"Amen."

Suddenly, a shadowy figure lunged from inside with a folding chair in hand. Using it, he or she smacked Greer and she toppled into Locke with a groan. He caught her and set them both right, but the figure was already sprinting through the rows of house trailers.

"You all right?" he asked Greer.

"Yeah. Let's go!"

Greer bolted from the area with Locke right beside her, but they soon lost the figure in the night. Greer bent at the waist, hands resting on her thighs. "I don't think that was a man. Frame was too slight and while the impact wasn't like being pelted with a stuffed animal, it wasn't as intense as the force behind a man."

Greer had noticed the shadow had been slender. Not as tall as Locke, but taller than her.

"Could be Jenna Dennison. She had time to

hurry over after we left her RV to talk with Bolt Masterson."

Greer's breath evened out and she headed toward the campers. "Could be," she said. "The height fit Star Jumper—the knife thrower's assistant—and Jewel."

He softly caught her elbow. "I can't put off heading to Rolling Hills any longer. You don't need to be here alone. It's too dangerous. Come with me. We can search the trailer more thoroughly as soon as I'm done. Promise."

Greer glanced toward Flip's house trailer. Heaving a sigh, she nodded. "Okay. I don't think whoever was in there found what they were looking for. I wish we had the manpower to put a deputy on the camper all night."

They hurried to Locke's truck. He opened the passenger door for her, then hopped in the cab. "I feel like I've been plopped down in the middle of one of my grandma's stories she watches on daytime TV."

Greer snorted. "It does feel like a soap opera. So many secrets. Criminal activities. And we've only skimmed the surface."

"You ready to chase some tornadoes?" Locke asked.

Greer was ready to face anything except a killer who was bent on making sure she didn't come out of this alive.

* * *

The smell of toast and coffee filtering into Locke's senses teased his eyes open. But his body and brain protested. After chasing an F1 tornado in Rolling Hills last night and all the old excitement it brought, they'd enjoyed eggs and bacon at an area diner. Locke's research team had shown up and they'd discussed the data recorded and talked about the worst twisters they'd ever been in. Thankfully for the surrounding towns, the twister dissipated before wreaking havoc, but there had been significant wind and hail damage.

By the time Locke and Greer had returned to her house it was nearly 3:00 a.m. He wanted to sleep this lazy Sunday morning away, but the sounds of clanging in the kitchen along with the rich aroma drew him off the couch.

He staggered into the kitchen. Greer was making toast and sipping juice. While she still had abrasions from previous attacks and soft purple lines of exhaustion under her eyes, she appeared to have more pep in her step than Locke. She was dressed in a cottony dress that reached her ankles. Bright summery flowers dotted it. Her hair was down and in soft waves around her face. "Where are you off to this early?"

"It's Sunday. I go to church."

"But we didn't get home until three. Aren't

you exhausted?" he asked, then suddenly his neck flamed. Home. This wasn't Locke's home. They weren't a couple. He wasn't sure what they were. If they were anything. Lines were blurring lately. "You know that you can miss a Sunday and not get sent to the fiery pits below, right?" This is why he never liked church as an institution. Too many dos and don'ts. Too many judgy people judging.

Greer set her juice on the granite countertop. "I didn't say it would. But I enjoy church and I could use some encouraging words and peace with everything going on."

Church itself had never brought much comfort to Locke. From the time he was little he was constantly reprimanded.

Sit still.

Quit fidgeting.

Stop doodling on the prayer cards.

Why can't you pay attention?

The list went on and on. Locke had failed at church. Why go to a place if he couldn't get it right when he was there? "I feel God's peace and comfort when I'm out in nature." Where he could dress how he wanted. Move freely and not be forced to stand still or follow strict rules.

Greer poured Locke a cup of coffee and handed it to him. "So do I. The Bible says that the heavens declare His glory. It only makes sense to feel His presence while in nature. But it also says not to forget assembling together, too. People coming together to worship is uplifting."

Locke sipped his black brew and shrugged. "Not when I went."

"I'm sorry you didn't have a good experience as a kid or teenager."

They hadn't talked religion or church much during their dating, other than that they were believers and grew up in church.

"Nothing fun about sitting on a hard pew listening to sermons you have no idea what they mean and being forced to sing songs that didn't make sense." But somewhere in all that Locke had felt a stirring in his heart. A stirring to accept Jesus as his Lord and Savior. It had been his grandmother who had helped him understand what it meant to be a follower of Christ, and she had helped him pray and ask God to save his soul.

"Well, our church has a special service geared to children. Get dressed and go. I'm sure they'll let you sit in on that one." She winked and buttered a piece of wheat toast.

"I just don't do church. I believe in God and I pray. I have a Bible." Sometimes he read it. Not as much as he should.

"I don't *do* church, either." Greer handed him two pieces of toast and set the butter in front of him, then pulled out a jar of strawberry jam and handed him that. Did she realize she was giving him his favorite jam or was that all she had? Something about the familiarity tugged on him.

"Church isn't something you do, Locklin. Church isn't a place. Not really. The church is a group of God's people. And my church is like family. They didn't judge me when I was unwed and pregnant but held a baby shower for me and brought me and Mama meals after Lin was born."

Locke would have helped. Would have been there. If he'd been informed and asked.

"And when Mama was sick, so many came by to pray, to just be here. To bring food. I have tons of gifts, texts and calls to be thankful for. And even now with what's been happening, I've had texts and friends like Tori and the Woolridges, who have stepped up to help us with Lin. That's church. Loving one another and rejoicing when others rejoice and weeping when they weep. I do life with my church family. I do not do church."

Greer's definition sounded pretty sweet. So unlike what he'd experienced, but then he had been a rowdy, fidgety boy with the attention span of a gnat. "Well, enjoy it then. I'm going to skip. I don't have a suit and tie, anyway."

"You're not Justin Timberlake. You don't have to wear a suit and tie. Jeans and a T-shirt are fine."

Locke chuckled and bit into his toast. "I'd rather not." However, the last thing he wanted to do was let Greer and Lin out of his sight. Even in church.

Her soft sigh didn't go unnoticed.

"But I'll go. If you don't mind being a few minutes late so I can get ready."

"You don't feel comfortable with us being alone, do you?"

"Not even a little."

He rushed to Lin's room and rifled through his bags. He glanced outside. That's where he experienced God. In the bright yellows, oranges and reds. In the towering oaks. The green of the grass. All in nature. The blue of the sky. The sparkle on creek water.

God was in the wildness of a whirlwind. Powerful and holy. He was in the tenderness of spring grass. The relief of a cool wind in the heat of summer. That felt like church. Open. Free. Unconfined. Reaching far and wide.

But Greer's words… Church wasn't a place— it was people. Doing life together. Locke did most of his life alone. His family would always be there for him—even if he was a total failure most of the time—and he used to believe Greer would be. Something in the marrow of his bones tugged—a call…to give it a chance.

He checked his watch and got a move on.

Then he and Greer drove to church. She called to ask Cindy to save them seats and keep Lin in the sanctuary. Anything could happen with a cunning killer on the loose and she must want all the extra time she could get with Lin. Locke could relate.

The sounds of a band playing came from the main sanctuary. A few people milling about smiled and welcomed him. No one glared that they were late, but better late than never.

A sudden case of nerves hit him. Last time he darkened a church door was four years ago and only because it was Mother's Day and Mama had asked him to come as a gift to her.

An usher with a bushy mustache and a crooked smile met him. "Can I help you find a seat?" he whispered through the band singing about an unstoppable God.

"Michael and Cindy Woolridge are saving us some."

"Gotcha." The usher led them to a section of plush chairs and they slipped down the aisle. Cindy spotted them first and hugged Greer. She nudged Michael, who was singing in a baritone voice and holding Lin. He grinned and passed Lin to Greer. Locke studied the words on the big screens flanking the stage. Upbeat. Full band. Congregants worshipping in all ways. Hands raised. Hands down.

Lin grabbed the sleeve of Locke's dressier T-shirt with the deep V and stole his attention. He reached for her and she instantly went to him, filling his heart with ease. This little girl already trusted him. Wanted him. More than anything he wanted to be her hero and not mess things up. He wanted her to always reach for him. Look up to him.

Greer smiled and closed her eyes as she sang the words. For the first time in days, true peace flooded her face, softening it. Evening out the worry lines. She'd need it, too. Inside the church it was calm and secure, but outside terror reigned and was coming for her.

After worship, Greer's pastor spoke about having an intimate relationship with God, the kind that Moses had—as a friend. Locke could get on board with that. He often talked to God. It was the whole organized church with their own rules—rules he'd never found in the Bible—that they expected people to adhere to. But in this church, he wasn't seeing any of those strict regulations.

People smiled, laughed and had even cheered on the pastor as he preached. No one scowled when small children cried or fidgeted, including Lin, when she'd gotten antsy. Maybe his past experiences had skewed his perception of what church should be. What it could be. What it very well might be.

After the service, he thanked the Woolridges for keeping Lin. Greer led him through the foyer, and several people stopped and made conversation, greeting him with sincerity and kindness. Greer carried the diaper bag and her purse while Locke kept Lin close to his chest, drool dripping onto his shirt. "What do you want for lunch, Locke?"

"I'm up for anything so I don't care. Should we take Lin out?"

"Restaurants will be super crowded and the traffic will be tight even in this tiny town. So I feel okay about taking her to eat with us. Tori should be home from her shift at the hospital after that, so I guess we go the long way around again."

Locke didn't feel like it would be a travesty to take her into one restaurant that was filled to the brim with diners. "Okay. We can go out."

"What sounds good?"

"I don't know. What sounds good to you?" Lin grabbed a handful of his hair and squealed. Kid had a serious grip. He gently pried open her fingers and released his hair from the prison of baby hands.

Greer sighed. "I don't know. Anything."

"Mexican?"

"No, I don't want that."

"You said anything." Same ole same ole. How many times had they had the food battle when they were together? Seemed like a lifetime ago and also like they'd never been apart. Locke wasn't sure what to make of that.

"Well, anything but that. How about down-home cooking? The Blue Bass café has a lunch-plate special on Sundays."

"Deal."

After buckling up, they headed to the Blue Bass café. Inside they found a booth in the corner. Greer grabbed a high chair and strapped Lin inside, then gave her some toys to occupy her. After ordering drinks and a one-meat-and-four-vegetable plate for Locke and the baked chicken and dressing for Greer, he leaned in. "I liked your church."

Greer smiled and dug through the diaper bag, pulling out a jar of carrots. "Good. I'm glad you did. I'm sure if you didn't travel so much—and you wanted to—you could find a good home church."

"Three out of twelve months isn't a lot, Greer."

"Sometimes you travel more and you said you wanted to travel all year round. Just go where the wind takes you." She turned to Lin, who was bouncing in her seat and eyeing the jar of mush as if it was roast beef and mashed potatoes laden with thick gravy, which happened to be part of Locke's lunch-plate order.

"I know I said that but it looks like the wind blew me into my daughter's life. When I'm not traveling for legit work, I'd like to be around to see her. We need to talk about this. It's not going to go away."

Greer spooned in a bite of carrots and Lin lapped it up. "You don't have to change your life for us, Locke."

That was the third time she'd made a comment similar to this. Like she was hoping he'd take the out she was tossing him and opt out of being a dad. If he stuck around, he was probably doomed to fail, but looking into Lin's little face—his very own image—he couldn't run for it. Wouldn't. "I want to."

"You say that now," she grumbled and gave Lin another bite. She was definitely a healthy eater. She'd almost cleared the jar and was banging on the tray, mouth wide open in anticipation of another bite.

Locke's dander rose but he inhaled and counted to five. "I do say that now. And I mean it now." He huffed and opened his mouth but was interrupted by Deputy Crisp and Deputy Garrison.

"Hey, how did the rest of the photo shoot go?" Adam asked.

"Well…could've been better." Greer told him what happened. "I'll turn in the report today."

Adam glanced at Locke but didn't speak. "I'm glad you're okay. My offer still stands."

"We're all good," Greer said.

Deputy Garrison harrumphed. "Just watch your back, Greer." He glanced at Locke, a measure of disdain in his eyes. No doubt Locke looked like the deadbeat dad who didn't care if he was in the picture or not.

Wait.

It hit him full-force. Greer's dad had flown the coop when she was little. Did she think Locke would, too? He itched to get to the bottom of this but the deputies didn't seem to mind infringing on their privacy. Adam seemed happy to, and Ben…well, he kept a wary eye on Locke, which stirred up a dose of irritation. Dude didn't know the whole story. What happened to not judging books by their covers and all that jazz? And the same could go for Greer if that was the connection she was making between Locke as a father and Greer's own dad. He might royally fail, but he wouldn't abandon his daughter. Not ever.

After lunch at the Blue Bass and letting Lin get a nap in, the day was over half-gone and Greer still hadn't been able to wrap her brain around Locke accompanying her to church and that he liked it. He'd gone to protect her, so he wasn't obligated to tell Greer he'd enjoyed it.

Greer hadn't been as faithful to God and church in her early twenties. Some might have even called her a prodigal. And Locke, too, for that matter. But now that she'd gotten her life back on track and God was in the center, she wanted Lin to have a godly father. Dad hadn't been big on religion or relationship, but Mama had always taken her and Hollister to church.

Playing house and church with Locke had given her a measure of comfort she couldn't afford. In a few days, he'd be leaving. Lin would quickly forget. Greer, not so much. Last night had been like old times. Racing against the weather together and eating at a greasy spoon in the middle of the night, adrenaline running through their systems. Too many emotions she'd forced into seclusion had sprung loose in her heart and opened her up for upcoming misery.

If Locke spent his entire downtime here in Goldenville, Greer feared she'd fall in love with him again and become as attached as Lin would—and be dependent on him. Then he'd leave to chase what he loved most, leaving them behind to face fear and loneliness. Greer didn't want to be his second best. And she sure as sunshine on a summer day didn't want Lin to feel second best. A girl needed her father's love and approval. She needed to know he'd move mountains to provide for and protect her. Greer had a gaping hole thanks to Dad tearing out her heart.

Locke's laughter and Lin's giggles floated from Tori's living room, squeezing her chest. Anyone who didn't know them would think they were a happy family. She longed for that. More now that it edged her life and teased her heart. She sighed and grabbed the diaper bag. A notification popped up on her phone.

Pausing at the door, she scrolled through the messages. Sweet! Someone wanted the old coffee table. Hello, sixty-five dollars. That would buy a pack of diapers and a can of formula. She hurried into the living room. Locke was lying on his back, raising Lin over his face in the air. Locke made airplane noises and "flew" her back and forth. She giggled and a string of drool hung from her open mouth. Before it reached Locke's face, he sat up and wiped it away with his fingers. Such a dad move. Greer felt the pang along her ribs. She was torn. "One day, little lovely, you'll have to stop doing that. Actually, never stop doing that. That'll chase all the boys away. No boys for you."

Greer leaned against the wall and wished she had her camera.

"Hey," he said when he caught her lurking.

"Hey. A woman from Rolling Hills wants to

purchase the coffee table. She's actually going to be in the area in thirty minutes. I told her we could meet at the park. Care to go by the house and help me load it and swing it over?"

"Will it fit in the back of your CR-V or should we take the truck?"

"Either is fine. I'm gonna go let Tori know we're leaving." She'd been giving them some space by hanging out in her bedroom.

"Okay."

Twenty minutes later they had the coffee table in the back of Greer's SUV and were headed to the park. "This is legit, right?" Locke asked. "You've done this before? Sold to people in neighboring towns?"

Greer backed into a spot closest to the entrance, like she told the woman she would in her private message. "A few times, yes. It's a public website."

"What time did she say she'd be here?" Locke asked.

"One thirty." Greer scoured the parking lot. "She's in a maroon Enclave."

"Did you charge a hauling-it-from-your-SUV-to-hers fee?" he teased.

She should have. Her bank account was sad. "No, I figured you'd be a southern gentleman and handle it."

Greer hopped out and popped the hatch while Locke unfolded from the vehicle.

Simultaneously, a crack sounded and a bullet crashed into the metal on her car, driving her heartbeat into overtime.

"Get down!" Locke bellowed.

Greer ducked, drew her weapon and scanned the parking lot. No signs of people.

Another bullet slammed into the trunk lid.

Greer scrambled to the driver's side but feared shooting into the woods. There were bike trails out there. Walking paths. She might hit someone.

Another bullet slammed into the car.

"Greer. Get in." Locke had made his way around the SUV and practically shoved her inside the backseat on the driver's side.

Locke jumped behind the steering wheel, staying low, and peeled from the lot, the hatch still open and the table falling out.

"Greer, tell me you're okay," Locke demanded, his voice shaky. He could have taken a bullet shoving her inside.

Would her own father have taken one for Greer? She didn't believe for one second he would have, then or now. He wasn't even around to do it. Her eyes burned. "No—no, I'm not hit."

The shooter came from the woods so there was no way he could have gotten into a vehicle and chased them down, but there were so many

secrets and carnival workers sticking together—
hiding things from them—Greer wasn't going
to take the chance and assume only one person
was at that park. She glanced out the rear window. No one seemed to be on their tail.

She'd never forgive herself if anything happened to Locke. He shouldn't have signed up
for this.

Once he hit Main Street, he slowed and parked
along the street. After surveying their surroundings, he spoke. "We're safe now, and I know
you're thinking it. I am, too."

Greer heaved a sigh, her head dizzy with
adrenaline. "Yep. Someone set me up." She
climbed in the front seat with Locke, beating
herself up mentally for not thinking it might be
a setup in the first place. Even if it did look legit,
she was better than this. Smarter than this. But
she'd been in such a panic since the attacks and
since Locke got to town. Not to mention sixty-
five dollars was a big deal to a single mama with
an infant. "I feel like an idiot."

Locke's arm came around her shoulders and
he tucked her into his chest for support and comfort. "The question is how would a carny know
you were posting items for sale on a website?"

"I also post the link on my Facebook page,
leaving it public. Anyone can see it if they visit.
I was trying to stretch the reach and sell this

stuff. If the shooter was keeping tabs on me, stalking me online as well, then it was a prime opportunity. But I feel like I'm not firing on all pistons and that's unacceptable. I should have anticipated this."

"Greer, don't beat yourself up. I only questioned it when we got here and didn't suggest leaving. I think between fear, chaos and utter exhaustion, giving yourself some grace is okay. Humans—even trained officers—make mistakes."

Locke always had a way of making her feel better. "I assure you, I won't be setting anything to public or using the online shop again. At least until we've caught this guy. If we can catch him. He's slippery." No one would come forward with any solid leads. The carnival would be gone come this Thursday. They'd pack everything in Wednesday night. Be gone by morning and the killer would get away scot-free…or would he even leave? What if he hid out and stuck around until he finished the job? "And I didn't say it, but we've been looking for a guy with a beard and mustache. What if that first night he attacked me he was in a really good disguise?"

Locke inhaled deeply and exhaled slowly. "That would explain no one matching his description and why he stole all your editing software and laptop. Originally, he may have invaded to snoop up on you, but he spied the software. He's clearly smart, so he probably assumed it was downloaded to your laptop, which is why he took it. He might have pieced together that you could use it to his disadvantage. Edit out a beard. A mustache. Change up his hair and facial features. Boom. You'd be able to identify who he really is."

Greer's stomach roiled. "This broadens our suspect list by a mile. Anyone could be the killer."

"Anyone who is skilled at throwing weapons and familiar with the fun house—which might be many carnival employees, but the knife-throwing skill has to be limited." Locke ran his hand through her hair, showing no urgency to release her from the embrace. "I think it's time we bring in some reinforcements, Greer. I know you want to be the brave one, and you are, but we aren't winning right now, darlin,' and he's become even more brazen. He hasn't hurt our daughter, but she's still at risk."

Our daughter.

First time he'd said that. It had been *his daughter* since he found out.

"I want to call my sister."

Greer pulled away. "Send Lin away with strangers?"

Locke shook his head. "I'm going to have her come here. That way we still have her close but can focus on finding this killer. You're being pulled in a thousand directions. Welcome to my daily brain-world." He chuckled.

"I don't want Jody to think I can't protect my own daughter." She didn't want Locke to think it, either. What if they used it against her somehow? No, they would never. Greer's deepest fears were running wild.

"Greer. You're strong, capable and fully able to keep our baby safe. So am I, but we need to call in backup. You'd do it if you were on duty and things got hairy, you know you would."

Locke made a strong point. "What if she can't come?"

"She's family. Family takes care of one another. No matter what. When things are bad, they drop it all to come."

Greer's burning eyes betrayed her and tears leaked. "My mama died. And…my dad left. He was never there for important events and milestones, and he was never there when I needed him. He didn't even call when Mama died. Didn't come to the funeral. And I needed him, Locke. I needed my daddy. But he didn't want or need me."

Locke brushed away her tears. "Greer. I'm so sorry. I'm sorry he was a perpetual no-show. He was the one who missed out. Not you, darlin'. And you have Hollister. I can call him. Have him come, too, if you'd like."

Hollister had a million things going on and she didn't want to involve another person she cared about—no matter how strong and skilled they were. "No, it's okay."

He tipped up her chin. "You may not have your father, but you have a whole host of townsfolk and church people who care about you and would bend over backward to be there for you. You said it yourself. You do life with them. I've seen it."

Greer touched his scruffy cheek. "I'm glad you're here, Locke."

"I am, too."

He held her gaze then slowly dipped to her lips.

A horn in the distance broke the mood. Locke blinked and licked his bottom lip. "Sorry. I—"

"No, it's all right."

But it wasn't. Nothing was. And Greer wasn't sure when it would be again. Locke cranked the engine and backed out of their parking space. As they pulled on to her street a small silver sedan sat in her driveway. Out on the porch, Hollister paced.

Well, she may not want to involve anyone else, but her big brother was here, anyway. Just like Locke said. Family dropped everything to help.

She stepped out of the vehicle. "What did I tell you?"

"Doesn't matter," Hollister said. "I'm here. If for nothing else than to clean out this garage and the attic." He glanced at Locke as he rounded the car. "Locklin."

"Hollister."

This was about to get interesting.

NINE

Locke stood in front of Greer's picture window, chewing at his thumbnail and bobbing his leg. He had entirely too much nervous energy coursing through his muscles. He'd called Jody and given her the crime-related news, then he'd asked her to fly in and help, and she'd said yes before he ever had the chance to tell her it was to babysit her niece, not to go all Wonder Woman on a killer. She'd said, "Say no more. Evan and I will be on the first flight out." He gave her the address and that was that.

Then he'd had a conversation with Hollister on the way to pick up Lin. Between the three of them, and Jody and Evan on the way, they felt having her at the house for a while wouldn't be dangerous. Hollister had informed him that Greer had finally come clean about not telling Locke about Lin and that his stay was indefinite. The more protection for Greer and Lin, the better, plus there were things around the house that Greer shouldn't have to handle alone. Then after hanging out a while, Hollister had left to visit a few old friends. Mostly he was giving them space for when Jody and his brother-in-law, Evan, arrived. Guess he trusted Locke to keep Greer safe or he wouldn't have left at all. And that felt good even if he hadn't been doing such a hot job. Greer had a few bruises and cuts to prove it.

Jody had called when they rented a car and, according to the time, she was about ten minutes away from Greer's home.

"Coffee, Locklin?" Greer softly asked.

He glanced at Greer standing barefoot in the kitchen doorway. "No, thanks." He didn't need the added caffeine. Lin smacked her exersaucer with a plastic block and bounced up and down. They should make those for adults.

"She's going to hate me, isn't she?"

"Jody? No. Besides the last person she hated, she married." He grinned. "No worries." She already had enough.

"*You* seem worried," Greer said.

He wasn't, but he was puzzled. "Greer, can I ask you a personal question? Like seriously deep."

Greer nodded and sipped her coffee, her wary eyes trained on his.

"You said your dad wasn't around when you

needed him. That you didn't want me in and out of Lin's life. She needed to be able to count on me. Do you...do you think I'll be a bad dad because I'll be like yours?" That wasn't fair.

Greer toed the carpet, looked anywhere but at him. Lin bounced like she'd never get to do it again. Locke crossed the room and dipped down to make eye contact with Greer. "Do you?"

A car in the driveway caught their attention. Jody and Evan.

This conversation wasn't over. Just on hold. "How do you want this to go down?" Locke asked.

"How do you?" Greer's eyes held fear. Uncertainty.

"I'll go out there alone. Then bring them in to meet Lin."

Greer grabbed his elbow as he headed for the kitchen. "I should do it. I kept Lin from you. From your family. I should have to face the music."

Three nights ago, Locke would have agreed. Been more than happy to let her march out there and tell Jody she'd kept her from being an aunt. Hurt her little brother. Jody had always mamahenned him as a child. Still tried. But three days felt like a lifetime ago. They'd been through eons of mess in seventy-two hours.

"You did face the music, Greer. You faced me."

"Because I had no choice."

"Is what it is. I got this one," he murmured. "Be right back." Locke went out the front door. Jody met him with a grin. Her hair was as blond as his was black. Her eyes weren't quite as blue as his, but close. She lunged from the rental and wrapped him in a hug. "You smell like baby shampoo, bro." Jody had a condition that heightened her sense of smell. It was a blessing and a nightmare at times. Of course she'd smell Lin on him.

Evan greeted him with a firm handshake. "How's the storm chasing, Locklin?" The man had never called him Locke to his face, not in all the years he'd known him.

"Busy."

"Okay, so we've relayed all information pertaining to the case to the rest of the team at Covenant Crisis Management, but we'll need more official details from Greer," Jody said. All business. But her eyes softened. "Things going okay with her? You getting along? Any answers to why she left you high and dry?"

Locke swallowed hard and glanced at the picture window. Greer was nowhere to be seen.

"I mean she has to have some kind of explanation." Jody held up her hands. "I told myself I wouldn't get up in arms, but she hurt you, Locke."

"I did." Greer's voice came from near the garage. Lin was secured to her hip. "And I'm sorry for that."

Jody spun around and stared at Greer, then at Lin. "How old is that baby? Did you step out on my brother?" she asked, her voice raised. Evan laid a hand on Jody's lower back and whispered something in her ear.

"Look closer, sis," Locke said.

Jody stepped toward Greer, studying Lin. Her eyes grew wide and tears bloomed in them. "You have a daughter?" she whispered to Locke.

"He does," Greer murmured. She'd come out to own up to her part and admiration swelled in his chest, but Jody could be a firecracker when she felt threatened or when she was angry. And something inside him needed to protect and defend Greer even though what she'd done was wrong. There was no defense. But those feelings were between him and Greer alone. They didn't need to extend to other members of the family.

"You kept—"

"Can we talk privately, please?" Locke asked. "Go on in the house. I'm right behind you."

Jody nodded and left Evan outside with him and Greer.

"You know how she can get when it comes to you," Evan said to Locke.

Very Mama bear. "I'm not seven anymore."

"I know," Evan said and walked over to Greer

and Lin. "She looks like you, Locklin. Be thankful it's working in her favor," he teased and slapped Locke on the back in a brotherly gesture. "Go talk to Jody. I'd like to spoil my niece if I'm allowed." Evan grinned and Greer's shoulders relaxed. He owed his brother-in-law big-time.

"She's going through stranger anxiety," Locke said.

Greer snickered.

"Well, she is!" Locke growled and rushed through the garage, hearing Evan's last words.

"You won't be scared of your uncle Ev, will you? No, you won't."

Baby talk. It happened to the best of them.

Inside Jody stood in the living room in front of the photo collage on the wall. She didn't look at him but she spoke. "You know how much I like Greer. I always thought she was the one for you. I was afraid you'd screw it up. Never expected it to be her."

Another reminder that he was a total letdown. Even if she was halfway teasing, the sting lodged in his chest. "Thanks?"

She grinned and hugged him. "Tell me what's going on."

After relaying everything that had transpired, from his and Greer's relationship, through to her witnessing a murder on Thursday, he sighed, collapsed on the couch and raked his hands through his hair. "I was in the middle of asking about her dad when you drove up. You said it yourself, I screw things up. I have my whole life. You were there when I told Mama I wasn't going back to school. Told her and Dad I wasn't following in the Flynn-Gallagher footsteps and joining the military or becoming a lawman."

Jody sat next to him and put her arm around his shoulder. "Do you want to be a dad, Locklin?"

"Honestly? Yes and no." He massaged the back of his neck. "No, because I can't bear to see eyes identical to mine radiating utter disappointment in me. And I never thought about it too much, but when I saw her, held her...something happened. I can't explain it. I wanted to be a dad. I am a dad. I've known her less than a week and I'm crazy in love with that child. And I'm crazy scared because the only thing I've ever done right is capturing a perfect photo of a storm."

Jody wiped a few tears and held his hand.

"I live in a camper most of the time. When I'm not traveling for the team, I'm traveling on my own in between bunking in my old room at home. I can't have a daughter live in a camper. She needs a school district and friends. Greer's given her that. A home. A life. A church."

"Locklin, good dads aren't perfect dads. Our

dad was awesome, but he wasn't perfect. He was overly strict and *über*-structured thanks to the military. It was his way or no way. And once he was out of the navy, he never missed any of our events or milestones."

"You feel that way because you were the golden child. You did everything perfectly. Joined the navy. The Secret Service. Private security. You never let him down. That's all I ever did."

Jody wrapped her arms around Locke and kissed his temple. "No, brother. He was proud of you. Always showing people your photos and telling anyone who would listen about his son who chased storms and had more talent in his pinkie finger than Daddy had in his whole body."

The back of Locke's eyes burned. "He never told me."

"No, and he should have. So you make sure and tell Lin every day how proud you are of her no matter what. You love her. Be there for her. That's what's going to make you a good dad. Not a perfect one. Campers, houses, school districts—all that can be worked out."

Locke had no idea that Dad had been proud of him. Talked good about him. All Locke remembered was everything he'd done wrong. But there had been good times. Good talks. Good advice. And when the rubber met the road, Dad was there for him. Pulling him out of ditches, hauling him out of trouble at a party in his teens.

"You make it sound easy," he said.

Jody hooted. "I'm no parent, but I know it's not easy. And while I'm at it, Locklin Shane Gallagher, you need to pull your spiritual act together. Because the best father to imitate is our heavenly Father. You love Lin like He loves and cares for us, and you'll be fine."

Jody had a point. "I feel like I've disappointed Him, too, Jode."

"No, Locke. You haven't. Believe me, I've been there. Carried all sorts of guilt and shame. You know my past. In all that mess, all that anger at God and bitterness, He never once thought of me as a disappointment. To Him, we're nothing but potential. You look at your baby and see you. It melts you."

"It does."

"And when God sees us—His babies, His children—He sees Himself. And it melts Him. He loves us no matter what."

They were made in the image of God. Locke had never thought of it like that. He loved Lin and nothing would ever make him not love her. And God loved Locke. He knew his ways and behavior more than anyone.

"I needed that. Now I need to convince

Greer that I can do this. Not perfectly, but I can do this."

"You're right. Because this baby is ours. All of ours. We're going to spoil her rotten and love the mess out of her." She pointed to the window. Outside Evan was flying Lin around like an airplane. "He'll have a pair of baby aviators on her by Wednesday."

"Maybe you should have one of your own."

Jody grinned. "Maybe we will." She laid a hand on her belly.

"Are you?"

"Not yet, but we decided last month it was time to start a family." She watched Evan outside. "Lin and ours could grow up together."

If Greer allowed it. She nearly had a coronary when he'd mentioned taking Lin away on trips and weekends to see his family.

"Greer called her friend Tori. She lives on a farm near the edge of town. You and Evan are welcome to keep Lin there. She has plenty of space."

"Great."

Locke hugged her. "Thank you."

"You're my baby bro. I've always got your back, but right now, I want to hold my baby niece. Stormie Lin. I love that Greer did that. Shows she didn't give all of you up when she left, Locke. Things might be salvageable between you two."

He whipped his attention in her direction. "First of all, I don't know if I can trust her again in that way."

Jody's expression soured. "If God can give me a second chance with the man I love after he cost me my job in the Secret Service, then He can give you a second chance with a woman who hid a child from you. You'll have to forgive her first and trust can be worked on. Find out the reason. That may help you with any decisions."

Jody had a point, but… "Secondly, I didn't say I wanted a second chance with Greer. I just want my daughter."

She gave him the "look" again. "Well, we'll see how it all plays out."

They walked outside and Jody smiled at Greer. Greer returned it. Two women speaking without words. Two women he admired more than anything. He hoped Lin grew up to be exactly like them.

Evan brought Lin to Jody. "She's going through stranger anxiety so…"

Greer laughed and shook her head.

Jody frowned. "Since when did you become a baby expert?"

"Twenty minutes ago. I'm a fast learner."

Smack talk and baby talk continued for another fifteen minutes or so, then they headed back inside for coffee and shoptalk.

It was time to catch a killer.

Or at the very least, stay alive and survive what may come.

Monday morning brought oyster-colored skies, a chill in the air and an unease to Greer's bones. Yesterday had her completely emotionally exhausted. Her nerves were already toast from the attacks that kept coming, and then dealing with Jody—the woman could be scary—but in the end, they'd made their amends. The rest of the evening had been spent talking about the case at hand and getting the computer analyst, Wheezer, involved on Jody and Evan's side since he'd just returned from his honeymoon. She kind of felt bad throwing this on him but that came with the job description according to Jody. He was going to dig into the victims and the suspects Greer and Locke had put together.

Marty Wise, Bolt Masterson and Rudy Dennison were at the top of the list. In that order. But somehow at least one woman was involved. It was a woman who had been in the camper the other night and nearly knocked them over—but that didn't mean she was in on the attacks or murders. She may have seized an opportunity to get evidence that might incriminate her. Who was the mystery woman? Jenna Dennison. Star Jumper. Jewel Pharelli. Or someone else?

On Sunday night, after ordering pizza and letting Lin get warmed up to Evan and Jody, which thankfully, she did—especially Evan—they'd driven over to Tori's and she welcomed Locke's family to stay for as long as necessary. After midnight, Locke and Greer had left Lin with her best friend and Jody and Evan. Hollister was bunking on an air mattress in Lin's room and working on the garage and attic—getting them cleaned out, organized—and going through Mama's things that Greer hadn't been emotionally able to.

Now, she was staring out the kitchen window at 8:00 a.m., sipping her brew and dreading another stormy day. According to Locke and the weatherman on TV, the last storm system had moved out, but an even bigger one was moving in between today and Wednesday night. New storms had swept in through the coast, hitting Mobile hard. No place in Alabama seemed safe. Greer was so over the rain and tornado watches. Where was the sunshine?

Locke entered the kitchen in jeans and a white T-shirt, his hair wet, wild and curling around the edges. He hadn't bothered to shave and a day's worth of growth graced his chin, cheeks and neck—a look that suited him too well. Her belly flip-flopped over and again. The fresh soap scent didn't help the crazy sensations doing the cha-cha all around her ribs and dancing into her pulse, spiking it.

"Morning," he said with a husky sleep-laced tone as he poured himself a cup of coffee. Their new routine. Until it wouldn't be. If that car horn hadn't sounded, Locke would have kissed her yesterday. Greer chalked it up to impulsiveness. They had loved each other once. It wasn't like they suddenly weren't attracted to each other anymore. Did that mean Locke had forgiven her? Wasn't mad anymore? Did you kiss people you were mad at?

Maybe. Love. Anger. All mixed together brought all sorts of confusing feelings. "How did you sleep?" she asked.

"That couch has seen better days, Greer. But I've also slept in worse conditions. So there's that." He half smiled over his mug, steam pluming in the air. "Hollister still snoozing?"

"Of course." Her cell phone rang. She glanced at it. "Deputy Garrison," she said to Locke and answered. "Hey, Ben, what's up?"

"I'm assuming you're up and at it this morning."

"At what? I'm technically not supposed to be on this case and the sheriff has me basically on leave." Which ate at her. She needed the money. "But, yeah. I'm up."

"Well, I thought you'd want to know the analysis came back on the trace evidence they got off your hands when you were attacked Thursday night."

"And?"

She put Ben on speaker. "Locke Gallagher is here with me and, considering the situation, I feel no need to keep this information from him."

"You'll tell him either way so…" His tone sounded irritated. Greer didn't care.

Locke sat up straighter, laid his forearms on the table and leaned in. Greer's heart picked up pace.

"According to the report, there was some trace evidence of an adhesive on your skin and on Mr. Gallagher's. It's the kind used to apply prosthetics."

As she'd suspected, someone had disguised his identity to keep other employees from recognizing him. The beard, the mustache, even the facial features could have been altered. No wonder they couldn't find anyone fitting the physical appearance perfectly.

Ben continued, "The maintenance uniform fibers didn't match the ones the carnival employees use now. But here's where it gets weird."

As if it hadn't been weird all along?

"Go on," Greer said.

"A guy in the crime lab doing the analysis remembered the fibers and adhesive found on you also matched a victim from another case a few years back that ended up going into FBI hands out of Birmingham."

Greer gaped at Locke while her insides twisted. "And?"

"And I did a little digging and made a call to someone I know in the Birmingham office, which is a mess right now with the tornado that blew in the other night. He did me a favor and sent the reports. Turns out the same adhesive and fibers were found on seven different women murdered and left in shallow graves in woods all over Alabama in the past ten years. The most recent out of Birmingham."

Greer shivered and lost her breath. "I want that report."

"I figured you'd say that."

A knock jolted her from her seat. Ben stood at the back door with the reports in hand. Greer hopped up and opened the door. "What on earth?"

Ben smiled and stepped inside. "Sheriff said to keep you out of the loop because you're stubborn and won't let the rest of us do our jobs, but I told Adam we had to let you know."

"Adam didn't want to tell me?"

Ben shrugged. "He thinks you have enough to deal with without being frightened further. But I think you need to know because this feels… like I said, weird."

Indeed. It was for Greer to decide. Not Adam, and it stung that he'd be okay with keeping this secret from her. She glanced at Locke. He sat with his arms folded over his chest. Greer took the report from Ben. "Grab a cup of coffee if you want." She perused the trace report and pondered the situation. If this guy had disguised his facial features and stolen her laptop and taken editing software, then he must believe that she had the ability and skill to use it to discover his true identity. Which means he knew he was recognizable.

Ben busied himself making a cup while Greer read over the files, her hands trembling as things became clearer on one end and muddier on the other. Locke stood and laid a hand on her shoulder, then took the information and studied it for himself.

"Victims were brunette, blue-eyed, and they'd all been to a carnival around the time of their murders." Locke frowned. "Greer, this changes things. You weren't just in the wrong place at the wrong time when a man was murdered by a random carnival worker. You stumbled upon a serial killer. One who has eluded law enforcement for at least ten years! No wonder he's been coming for you with a vengeance. He has so much more to lose."

Sinking to the chair, Greer nodded and whispered, "I know."

Locke continued skimming the information. "Well, I was hoping it'd be easy and it would only be one carnival in common with all victims, but it wasn't. It was multiple carnivals. Some within just months of each other, but mostly about a year apart."

"Is this guy tracking carnivals and pretending to be an employee to get in and out?" Greer asked. "No one would pay attention to a guy in a maintenance uniform. And with the facial disguise, if they did describe him to the police, it wouldn't be accurate. He fooled me."

Ben returned to the table. "He could have easily hopped from one carnival to another as a worker. After he murdered a victim, he could wait for a stretch of time—so not to rouse suspicion—then leave and find work at the next. The murders are spaced out. It's not a stretch to consider his employment at each carnival where a victim had attended."

"But surely the police and even the FBI investigating these cases searched each and every carnival for the one person who had been employed by each one of them. Right?" Locke asked. "Even if some time elapsed. If it were me, I'd do a search using the time line from the date of the carnival through six months after. There'd have to be a pattern."

"You ever consider law enforcement?" Ben asked.

"I've been around it a time or two." He smirked.

Greer groaned and rubbed her temples. "Not every carnival is reputable. We've been over this. They don't require background checks. Some have the shoddiest of files. We know firsthand they keep secrets. If a carnival got wind that one of their own was a—a serial killer, they'd shred the records, keep their mouths shut. It might put them out of business. Surely it would ruin their reputation. They promote family-friendly entertainment!"

They sat in silence. The truth permeated the room like an invisible pillow suffocating them as they soaked it all in.

When this carnival ended it wouldn't be over for Greer. The stakes were too high. The killer had too many secrets that could be exposed.

He was going to come at Greer until he succeeded.

She would not cry. Would not fall apart. She couldn't. "Can I see that report again?"

Locke handed it over and Greer carefully read through it all once more. "The wounds all match the same kind of knives that killed Flip and Tiny

Tim and the one thrown at me." She heaved a breath, feeling nauseated.

"Is the FBI coming to Goldenville?" Locke asked.

"Be a few days due to the storms, but before the carnival uproots, I suspect an agent will come in to assist."

They could use the help. Greer would welcome them. "Ben, will you keep me posted on the ballistics from the park yesterday?" Greer had called it in. Techs had come out and searched for evidence, bullets and casings. Maybe they could get a match to a gun. Track him that way.

"Sure thing."

Good. Obviously, Sheriff Wright was fine with her being out of the loop and Adam, too. Speaking of… "Where is Adam today?" Greer asked.

"Worked a double. He's off."

She wanted to call and give him a piece of her mind, but she wouldn't. Adam was only trying to protect her. Like she'd been trying to protect Lin by not revealing the truth to Locke. But had she been protecting her? That was the new nagging question.

"I need to get back to the station but I'll keep you in the know." Ben pointed at the files. "Copies. You're welcome."

Thankfully Ben was being super cooperative. She'd have to bake him a cake or something.

"Where does Tiny Tim fit in? Why would a serial killer take out Tim or Flip? They don't fit the victim profile."

"They must have seen or known something they shouldn't. Marty Wise was right. I don't think Tim was killed over drugs. Not now that we know a serial killer was probably his murderer."

"Did Marty know because of a good guess or because he's the killer?"

"That I don't know," Locke said. "I'd like us to give this new information to Jody. She can pass it along to Wheezer. He can dig deeper and blur some legal lines." Locke grinned. "I'm not looking for admissible evidence, I'm looking for who might have worked all these carnivals in the last ten years."

"I want another crack at Flip's camper. And to talk to Jenna. While I don't believe Tim's death was drug-related in light of the new information, we can't rule it out for certain."

If they could find solid evidence, they might finally get the upper hand.

If not… Greer feared what may come.

TEN

Cumulonimbus clouds stretched like fluffy walls along the dappled horizon. The sun had been held hostage behind them, mirroring the somberness Locke had been feeling since Deputy Garrison had swung by Greer's almost two hours ago. The news that a serial killer who had stabbed at least seven people before—nine, if Flip and Tiny Tim counted—had set off a wave of nausea all through Locke.

Jody and Evan assured them if a link could be found, Wheezer would find it and that this was to be given top priority at Covenant Crisis Management. He would cross-reference employees past and present who had worked the fun houses, were skilled at knife-throwing and had been maintenance workers, even though it was likely the killer wasn't a legit maintenance employee presently. Surely with all that information, someone was bound to surface.

But when? Time was slipping through their fingers.

Locke hated having Greer back on the carnival grounds. Somewhere, a deranged killer who was skilled in murder and targeting prey was lurking. He glanced at Greer, touched his concealed Glock and draped his arm around her shoulders. As long as he was living, no one was going to hurt this woman. No. One.

Music had already started up and as they approached the games and rides, a few workers were setting up for another day. Wind whipped plastic tent walls and picked up empty cotton candy tubes, popcorn boxes and cups, blowing them across the asphalt.

The air smelled stale. Locke glanced up. Lighter streaks of gray slashed across the sky. Drops of rain scattered the pavement. *Uh-oh.* "Run!" Locke hollered and grabbed Greer's arm as the sky dropped hail the size of marbles.

Greer squealed and Locke jerked her a few feet to the carousel. With the covering, they'd be safe to wait it out. Hail could be dangerous. He had several scars from stitches to prove it.

The ice crashing on the metal dome above them was deafening. They stood in a sea of horses and unicorns as pebbles of ice littered the concrete.

A fair had come to town when they were in

college and he'd taken her. It had been their third date. He'd known on their first date he wanted to spend all the time he could with her. Greer was special. Tough but tender. Strong but completely feminine. Brilliant but not lacking in common sense.

Greer had jumped on a pony and Locke had stood beside her. Up and down. Up and down. About the fourth down, he'd kissed her, and when the horse soared back up, he'd hopped on back, not breaking the kiss. No, he'd fallen headlong into it until the ride ended, and even then, the carnival workers had to clap and whistle a few times to bring them back to reality. Because the kiss, the moment, the sensations had been every bit out of this world.

But that was a long time ago. They'd been a little younger. And a lot in love.

Greer must have noticed him gazing at her. She peered into his eyes, cheeks a shade pinker than they usually were. She gripped the pole connecting the white horse to the carousel. "It's been a long time since I've been on one of these."

"I haven't been on one since you."

"Same," she murmured through the clanging of hail above.

"I loved you, Greer. So much."

Her eyes filled with moisture. "I know. I loved you, too."

Locke cupped her cheek, stroking her soft skin with his thumb. He searched her eyes. Recognized the longing and the uncertainty. Too much uncertainty going on these past few days. Unhurriedly, he met her lips—with anticipation, as if he'd never once kissed her before. This felt brandnew but familiarity teased the edges of his senses.

He didn't press for more. Just a slow springtime dance. No reason to rush. Time, in this instant, was on their side, stretching out so they could savor the sweetness of one another. How was it in just a kiss Greer could dizzy his brain in such a wonderful way, make him feel heroic—like he could do anything, be anyone— and also convince him that he was hers alone? Special, completely acceptable, the way he was. In all his wildness. All his energy—right now he was deliberately putting all of it into this kiss.

He would fight for her. With her.

In this moment, he was safe and sound. He wasn't angry or bitter. He'd missed her so much. Not just kissing her like this. But her. Greer. The woman who had taken him by surprise and rocked his world. The woman who had shown him unadulterated love.

He pulled away and blew a slow but heavy, long breath and rested his forehead on hers. Hail turned into hard rain. "Now what?" he whispered. He couldn't deny his feelings in that kiss.

They'd surfaced and betrayed him. Or shone light on what he kept telling himself. He cared about Greer. More than he wanted to or should.

All day long, Locke could say he was only in this for Lin. To keep her safe and to keep Greer safe for Lin. But that wasn't the whole truth. That kiss was.

She forced space between them, but he noticed her wobbly legs, spied the rosy glow on her face and glazed eyes. It had affected her, too.

Thunder rumbled. A streak of lightning came as a reminder that storms were dangerous. What was brewing between Locke and Greer came with its own dangers as well.

Greer pushed a stray hair from her face. "You asked me if I thought you were like my dad."

Usually it was Locke chasing squirrels, not Greer. But he'd asked, "Now what?" so he'd let her go around the mountain to tell him. Dread pooled in his gut.

"I do. I know you are," she said quietly. "He used to take us on picnics, skating, to the coast. We'd spend time playing ball, cards and riding bikes. My dad was fun. He was always on the go, always had exciting adventures awaiting us. I can remember my mama laughing and saying, 'Jim, slow down. You're going to wear me out right along with the kids.' Dad would laugh with her, sweep her in a big circle and kiss her and say, 'Maggie, we can rest when we're dead.'"

Locke would have liked Jim had he not walked out on his family, not convinced Greer that Locke was exactly like him in that way. "Okay. I admit, I may have said something along those lines, but how will that make me a bad father?"

Greer leaned her head on the white metal pole poking out from the horse. "I loved my dad. He hung the moon. Could do no wrong. But when I got a little bit older, I noticed the arguing with Mama. The blowing out the door and being gone for hours. Sometimes the whole weekend. Until the night it got really bad. Hollister and me huddled in his room under the covers to muffle the yelling and sobbing but it did no good. I'll always remember that fight. Those last words."

"What last words, Greer?" Locke needed to understand. To figure out how to convince Greer that he needed and wanted to be in Lin's life.

"Dad told Mama that she'd trapped him. She got pregnant with Hollister and they had a courthouse wedding. A year later, she got pregnant with me. Dad said she did it both times to trap him. He was sick of it and wanted to live his own life. He'd never even wanted to be a dad. It was his time to go where he chose and do what he wanted...and not be tied down and trapped to 'this house, to you and the kids.' It was a prison."

Greer wiped stray tears on the back of her hand. "I was a prison to my own father. By existing, Locke. He never intended on having me. Never really wanted me. I guess he thought he did at first because of the fun times…but he was only happy and laughing when we were playing. But there's more to life than playtime. Being a responsible parent means sacrificing adventures to afford to pay bills and buy Christmas gifts. It means putting the children first and not because we have to, but because we want to. I'd go with one pair of jeans and a shirt the rest of my life if Lin has all she needs. Do you understand, Locklin?"

He clenched his teeth. Bit back the frustration and tried to understand the deep place Greer was coming from. She wasn't talking to him as a rational adult. The abandoned and rejected child was leading this charge, riding on a big stallion named Fear. "Greer, I admit I love fun. I love to have it, do it and search for it. But I know how to be a responsible adult. I have bills and I pay them. I'd have been caring for Lin financially had I known about her. I work with scientists for months and help with research. The only reason I don't have my own place is I'm gone so much I can't justify paying rent or a mortgage. I know how to meet deadlines. Yeah, I struggle with feeling antsy. I lose my train of thought and I should have stock in Post-it notes because

I forget sometimes with so much going on in my brain. But I'd never forget to love my daughter."

"Locke, you were starting a new and grand adventure. You hate being boxed in. Tied down. You can't even be still for thirty minutes. How can you buckle down for thirty years?"

That was fair. And true. "I could." Couldn't he? "I won't abandon Lin."

"I'm sure my father thought that same thing. Until he realized he couldn't do it. Then he left us and I've had to live with those words and that guilt. I didn't tell you about Lin because I couldn't bear it if she had the same hurts. That I let those hurts into her life. Especially knowing you never planned for children."

Locke gaped and shook his head. "I wouldn't have left you." But it wouldn't have been fair to her. To refuse her kids…didn't matter now. There was no room for what-ifs.

Thunder rumbled again and the wind knocked over a plastic trash can. "What do you want, Greer?" His own fear rose to the surface. Fear that Greer would ask him to walk away for good. That was something he could not, would not, do.

"You and I, Locke, we're like this carousel. We go round and round hoping we'll make it somewhere, but we won't. You would have married me and settled down and eventually resented us. You say you wouldn't have but I know you would." She held up her index finger and made circular motions. "Round and round. Getting nowhere. And I can't have a dad swinging into Lin's life on occasion, and less and less the older she gets. She needs a father who is here. Full-time. Never leaving. Can you do that?"

His stomach bottomed out. He had two months to fulfill by contract. Greer was giving him an ultimatum. Live here in Goldenville. Be a full-time dad to Lin. Be nothing to Greer. Do what for a living?

"You hesitated. That says it all."

Did it?

She stepped out into the drizzle and headed for Flip's camper. Locke followed. "You're not being fair. Greer, this whole your-way-or-the-highway is what's boxing me in. Not Lin." He was going to have a panic attack.

"But you admit you feel boxed in. You can't do it, can you?" She nodded with resolve. "You can't settle down, or settle in." She sniffed and wiped a few more tears. "I'm okay with it, Locke. I'm over you. Been over you. But I needed you to see the truth and now you do, don't you?"

Did he? Locke was so confused he wasn't sure he could tell her what direction was up or down. She was right but she also had to be wrong. Locke couldn't ever abandon or leave Lin. But he wasn't sure he could walk into a Monday-through-Friday business and sit at a desk for forty hours a week, either. The idea already choked him. But he also wanted to be a part of Lin's life and dragging Greer to court to fight for weeks and months and shuffling Lin around—that didn't seem right, either, though he knew scads of kids who had and they'd made it through okay. He raked a hand across his face. "I…" He swallowed. "I guess I do."

Disappointment drenched Greer's face, lingering in her eyes. "Come on."

He trudged behind her to Flip's camper, Locke's heart squeezing with every step. Emotion clogging his throat. Was he losing his daughter? Had he…had he inadvertently agreed to that? Was he going to have to leave Goldenville in a few days knowing he had a baby girl that he couldn't see because he'd hesitated to admit he could buckle into a desk job or something? He'd let Greer down and hadn't even meant to. He'd let his daughter down, too.

He shook it off as they approached Flip's little house trailer. He'd try and sort things out when he had time to think clearly and focus.

Greer pointed inside. "I'll take the right side. You take the left."

"Okay." She was calling all the shots, anyway.

Greer pulled at the linoleum floor tiles to see if any were loose. Flip might have hidden something underneath. It was hard to concentrate on the task. Less than forty minutes ago, Locke's impulsive side had overridden his level head and he'd kissed her into oblivion. It had erupted thousands of feelings she'd weighted down with justification. But in that kiss, there was no possibility of Lock abandoning Lin—or Greer. That kiss had felt like a man who wanted to stay. Needed to stay. Like a man who needed Greer to survive. And leaning into him had erased all her stress, her fears, her anxiety, and filled her with a sense of calm. A sense of belonging. That wasn't a man who kissed haphazardly. It was strategic. Deliberate. Intense.

But then it all fell apart when he'd claimed she was hemming him in. She was trying to help him see what the future would be like if he came back and inserted himself into Lin's life full-time. There was no revolving door. It was in and all the way in. The look on his face—the panic, fear…dread. It had undone every sweet and wonderful thing the kiss had birthed.

Because Locke now knew what Greer already did. He. Could. Not. Give. Everything.

And she needed everything.

No. Lin did.

A tear slipped through again and she hurried and swiped it before Locke noticed, but he was pretty preoccupied with digging through the drawers under the bed.

Truth was Greer had emotional needs, too. But she couldn't expect Locke to meet them. They weren't a couple. The kiss didn't change that. Didn't change that her guard had to go back up in order to protect her. Briefly letting it falter couldn't keep it down.

"I can't find diddly-squat, Greer," Locke groused. "Either this guy is ridiculously good or he didn't have anything to prove the accusations he slung at these people."

Greer was beginning to think the same thing. "I'm not ready to throw in the towel yet," she said as she felt along the back of the bench that housed the pull-out couch.

Locke grunted.

"That wasn't a barb, Locklin." She wasn't subtly alluding to him throwing in the towel at some point in regard to Lin.

"I don't want to talk about anything personal right now, Greer. I want to try and keep focused on this one thing. This one enormous thing. I can only handle one enormous thing at a time, okay?"

"Okay," she muttered.

Locke popped up, eyes wide as if a lightbulb had lit up his brain. "Where's the pull-out storage compartment?" He sprang out the door and hauled it to the back end of the camper. "Bingo."

Greer stood at a distance. "You think they forgot to look in there? I'd look there first."

He opened the hatch, then shoved his hands inside the cubby area, feeling around. He knocked on the wall. "Aha!" His crooked grin lit up his face, creased his dimple in his right cheek. With a little force and a grunt, he ripped off a panel and tossed it on the ground. He shined his cell phone's flashlight inside. "Bingo times two, baby!" He hoisted a large rectangular metal box from behind the false back. He dug in his pocket and retrieved a pocketknife. After a little finagling he had the box unlocked.

Greer hurried over. "I can't believe it. You did it."

"Amazing how I can surprise you." He gave her a knowing look but she batted it away. She couldn't take a chance on him, couldn't risk her heart or Lin's even if deep down she desperately wanted to. Over and over all she could hear were her father's words, and a fresh wave of excruciating pain and horrible terror swept over her. If she could get over the fear… But she'd tried. She'd recited scriptures about God being a Father to the fatherless. About perfect love and how it cast out all fear. And yet…she continued to battle the paralyzing fear.

"Hands up," a husky, rough voice said. From behind the other side of the camper a large masculine figure aimed a gun on them. "Don't think about getting wise, either. Hands up now or I'll shoot."

Slowly Greer raised her hands. Locke followed suit. Now would not be a good time for him to give in to his impulsive side.

"You, slide that box over and don't be funny about it or I'll put one in the boyfriend. I may do that, anyway."

"That seems rude," Locke quipped.

Greer shot him a dirty look. Now was not the time to be cheeky, either. She slid the box over.

"Toss the guns. Both of ya."

Locke sighed and chucked his gun. Greer followed suit. "Now, get inside the camper."

He wasn't going to take her? Wasn't going to shoot them both right here and now, with no one around? This couldn't be the serial killer. But who was it?

Greer inched toward the camper with her hands up and Locke moved in front of her, shielding her as they backed into the camper and closed the door.

"I don't like this guy," Locke mumbled and locked the camper door, peering through the filmy window.

The guy snatched the box and darted behind

the camper, then sprinted toward the carnival. Greer busted out of the camper, grabbed her gun as Locke grabbed his and they raced after him. They had to get that box. It held the key to the killer and to the murders, but the thief had vanished into the sea of campers and games. Greer stomped her foot and cried out. Not again. "That was our one advantage." She balled her fists and clenched her teeth.

Locke came to her side. "I know." No encouragement. There was none to be had right now. They were losing hard and fast. Glancing up, he whistled. "But that wasn't the serial killer. We'd be dead if it had been. That was someone who wanted evidence."

"I was thinking the same thing. We gotta find that box!"

"Not right now. We need to move. Thunderheads are scrolling fast." On cue, hefty gusts of wind smacked against them and the sky suddenly blackened. They rushed to the truck and jumped in.

"Locke, it's Jerry."

Locke pressed the button on the radio. "I'm here, Jerry."

"Damaging winds and possible tornado spotted in the Rolling Hills area again. I'm gonna need you to jump on it."

"Roger that." Locke looked to Greer. "Care to—"

Greer's cell rang and she answered. "What's up, Adam?" Adam, who wanted to keep the fact a serial killer was after her a secret.

"We need all hands on deck. Funnel clouds were spotted about fifteen miles south of Magnolia Trailer Park. We need help evacuating them to the shelter."

Guess he'd been called in after all. "Okay. I'm on my way." She hung up. "I need a ride to the station. I can't go with you. But I'll be fine." She buckled up as Locke drove from the lot, the wind shaking the truck.

Trees swayed and the weeds in the fields on either side of them were flattened like pancakes. "Just be careful. Call me when you're done and everyone—including yourself—is safe." Locke tightened his grip on the wheel and peeked at the sky. Rain broke through the nebulous clouds. He switched on his wipers and turned on his lights. "Where's the shelter?"

"About a mile from Magnolia. State money provided funds to build several throughout Alabama. Basement and small room with a ham radio. Someone from search-and-rescue volunteers to man it."

"I wish more towns had them. I read about Tennessee providing funds for shelters, too, and one in Mississippi." Locke pulled up at the station. "Please be safe. The weather and…other things going on… I—I gotta go."

"I gotta stay." Wasn't that their lot in life. She was staying behind and he was always leaving. "I'll be safe." She jumped out and raced inside. She grabbed a Jenkins County Sheriff's Department raincoat, slipped into a pair of rain boots and donned a deputy ball cap. Ben rounded the corner in his uniform and raincoat and hat. "What are you doing here?"

"Adam said all hands were on deck."

"They need to be. Follow me. We may have to evacuate with cars, too. First Community Church has drivers and vans ready to go." He tossed her the keys to her deputy's car.

Greer caught her keys and followed Ben. Rain poured in stinging drops as Greer raced to her car, flipped on her lights and squinted at the road in front of her. Most of the roads were clear of drivers, but not debris and limbs and branches.

She made her way to Magnolia. A tree was down at the front entrance. She drove around to the east side and hit the radio. "This is Deputy Montgomery. Request location to clear."

"Northeast quadrant," Ben called back. "Not everyone wants to go willingly."

"Roger that," Greer said and pulled slowly to the northeast side of the trailer park. These homes were death traps and most residents were elderly or disabled citizens. Some single mamas with small children. "I don't see any evacuation vans. ETA, please."

"Two minutes," he said over the radio.

She parked and jumped out, her rain boots landing in a deep muddy pothole. She trudged to the first trailer and knocked. When it opened, a woman with a cigarette and a baby on her hip scowled. "Officer?"

"Tornado has been spotted about twenty minutes away. We're evacuating. Gather up some belongings, one bag, and we'll get y'all to the shelter. When you see the van pull up, get in."

The woman nodded, then Greer went to the next door and the next. Most residents complied, though they didn't have pleasant words about the weather. Neither did Greer. Rain didn't let up. Thunder cracked so loud, Greer felt it in her chest, and the lightning was blinding. Bikes, tricycles, cheap lawn chairs blew from one yard to another. Greer ducked as a whiffle-ball bat blew straight for her.

Trailers rocked like boats in a tempest and the sparse yards flooded with muddy water.

Folks were making a run for it and climbing inside the two fifteen-passenger vans that had pulled up. Looked like more than one church was coming to the residents' aid.

"How you looking, Greer?" Ben asked.

"Two trailers left. One van has already exited the park."

"I'm on my way behind the evacuated residents on the south side."

"Right behind you," Greer said and sprinted to the second-to-last trailer. No one answered and she moved on to the last one.

"Go away," a shaky, elderly voice called.

Greer hit the radio button on her shoulder again. "I need the resident's name for two-thirty-one Apple Blossom, Magnolia."

Dispatch answered. "Hazel Camco. Seventy-four. Widowed."

Greer knocked again. "Ms. Camco, there's a bad storm. Possible tornado. We're evacuating. It won't be for long. Please come with me."

"No." The door opened. "I'm not leaving Fifi or Peppy."

The smell of cat urine and kitty litter whacked Greer's senses and did a number on her gag reflex. "I'm sure Fifi and Peppy will be okay. I'm worried about you." A huge limb cracked and fell onto the roof of the trailer next door and the door swung open, barely hanging on its hinges. Greer grabbed her ball cap and mashed it farther onto her head. "Ma'am, please."

"I'm only coming if my cats come."

Great Scott! "Okay." Greer stepped inside the

meager home. Might smell like cats but the place was meticulous. "Where are they?"

"They're cats. And scared." She tossed her a frown. Great. Greer did not have time for a game of feline hide-and-seek. After an eternity of searching and four scratches, along with a whole lot of irritation, Greer had the woman and her fraidycats rounded up and in the van. She waved them off and dashed toward her car. The van stopped and honked.

Greer splashed through the muddy potholes. Limbs were down in front of the van. She and the driver moved them and then Ms. Camco hollered out the door, "I need my purse. It's on my kitchen table. I have to have it! It has my medication!"

Oh, this *woman*. "I'll bring it to the shelter." She turned to the driver. "All y'all got to go. Now. Get safe. I'll be right behind."

She darted for the trailer. Greer was drenched from head to toe, but she'd grab the purse and do one more sweep. Lots of parents left their kids—some of them very young—in order to go to work. One might be hiding and afraid. The wind pressed against her and she had to lean into it to move forward.

Suddenly, she was knocked to the ground.

ELEVEN

Had something blown into her? Greer opened her eyes.

The killer! Dressed from head to toe in black. Black hood and ski mask. Greer went for her gun, but he held it up. "Looking for this?" he asked in a husky whisper. He slung her gun across the yard. "You won't need that." He unclipped her radio and chucked it, too, then he pulled his knife and held it to her neck. "No one to hear you scream." He grabbed her hair and dragged her through the mud and into Camco's trailer.

Greer screamed and tried to grab onto anything, including the door frame, as he hauled her up the two stairs. She kicked and wailed. But the park had been evacuated. The storm was loud and obnoxious. And she had no way to call in help.

He must have followed Locke and Greer from the carnival to the station, then tailed Greer here, and waited. Bided his time until he could have her alone. Or he had a police scanner and had guessed she might be here.

Inside, he slung her onto the couch. The man was impressively strong, but Greer wasn't going down without a fight. As he lunged on top of her, she kicked him square in the chest. All that kickboxing had given her thighs some power. He lurched backward and she sprung up and raced for the door. She needed to be out in the open. This place was too narrow.

If she could get to her car...

The killer growled, cursed and grabbed the back of her jacket, ripping the light fabric down the middle. She fell back against his chest and elbowed him in the sternum, but she knew she'd never make it outside, and if she didn't do something...she'd end up like those poor other women. Greer had read the reports, knew exactly how they'd died.

She spotted Ms. Camco's knitting on the cabinet by a cold cup of tea. She grabbed one needle as his arms came around her and he hauled her back into the living area. Greer thrashed and reared back her head, preparing to butt him, but he was too quick for that and he threw her to the ground. Her head slammed onto the floor, jarring her. His black gloved hand wrapped around her throat. As he brought the knife out with his other hand, she plunged the knitting needle into his shoulder. He wailed.

She wiggled free, jumped up and leaped out the door.

His roars sent shivers down her spine. If he wasn't infuriated before, he was now. Greer slogged through the mud and puddles, hurdling lawn furniture, grills and other sorts of outdoor equipment as well as fallen limbs and branches as she raced to her car.

By now he was right behind her. Her pulse pounded and her hands shook uncontrollably. She made it to her car and jumped inside, locking the door. She went to crank the engine but the keys were missing.

She glanced up.

He stood in front of her car dangling her keys in one hand through the rain-blurred windshield. In the other hand he held a throwing knife.

No. No. No.

Greer's doors were locked, but she couldn't stay in here forever. She searched the car for her rifle, but it must still be in lock-up. She hadn't had time to sign for the release of it—protocol before each shift. When she glanced up, he was gone.

The windows were beginning to fog. Her heart galloped at breakneck speed. Where did he go? Did he leave? Was he waiting? Her breath came in shallow pants as she darted her gaze around the perimeter, but she was almost blind to everything outside the car now.

Rain pelted on the roof.

The wind howled.

Click.

She snapped her head toward the passenger door. The lock had popped up. She squealed and leaped over, smashing it down. He was toying with her, crouching down low. She held her hands on the lock and tried to look below, to see him. Fear filled every vein in her body, rocketing through her.

Click.

She gasped and jumped back over to the driver's side, smashing down the lock and holding it. How long could she play this game? Was he creeping along the ground back toward the passenger side? He'd know not to mess with the backseat or he'd be stuck inside.

At some point, he'd win. Get inside. Get her out. She had to swallow the terror and go on the offensive. She slowly slid over to the passenger side, trying not to rock the car or give away her location inside. If he was crouched low, then he couldn't see her, either. When he unlocked the door, she made her move, and instead of re-locking it, she thrust the door open, hoping to knock him down and make a break, but he was crouched on the back-passenger side, so the door missed him completely.

He snatched her by the coat collar and yanked her out. She grabbed a handful of sludge and slung it in his eyes, then sprung to her feet and raced across the mud. Lights flashed ahead and she froze, looked back.

The man in black had vanished.

"Get in!" Locke called.

Locke! She'd never been more thrilled to see him. She raced toward his truck and jumped inside. "I thought you had to go?" She fell against him and he wrapped his strong arms around her, squeezing.

"I do what I want, remember? And I wanted to check on you."

He smelled like rain and soap. Like safety and promise.

"Funnel never touched down." He pulled back, cradled her face in his warm hands. "What happened?"

She'd tell him. She would. But right now, she needed to catch her breath and simply feel the security of being in Locke's presence, his arms. Greer fell against him and he held her until her breath steadied and she could explain what happened. "I need to find my gun and radio."

"Greer, I'm so thankful you're a tough, brave woman. A fighter. I don't think my ticker can take much more." He groaned and sighed, combing his hair with his hands. "Okay, let's get your gun and radio. I called Jody on my way over to check on them and Lin. They were in the storm cellar at Tori's."

"Good." She'd check on Hollister, who she'd begged to go back home. But he insisted on getting Mama's stuff cleared out and the garage organized. Greer read between the lines, though. Hollis wanted to be nearby for Greer's sake. She had no doubt he was safe.

They hopped back out in the thunderstorm and found her gun and radio. She called in she was safe and heading into the station. Back inside Locke's truck, he eased from the road that cut through the middle of the trailer park.

"Did he say anything to you, Greer?"

"Nothing of importance. I didn't recognize his voice but it felt like he might be masking it, like I said before. Batman-ish." Greer leaned her head back against the seat. She felt like she'd been run over by a truck. "He's strong. Really strong, Locke."

Locke handed her a bottle of water. "Here."

She drank deeply, nearly half of the bottle, and sighed. "Take me back to the station. I need to give this information to the sheriff. Fill out a report." She shook her head. "If I'd have come in to work as a deputy, not been taken off duty,

I'd have checked out my extra weapons from the locker for the patrol car. I was helpless inside there." She fisted the side of the door. "Makes me so mad."

Between debris in the road and limbs and full-on trees blocking them, it took almost forty minutes to get back to the station. They ran inside since the rain hadn't let up. The winds had slowed down. According to Locke's satellite they were now at ten miles an hour, not seventy. Inside, Ben stood with a cup of coffee. His eyes grew wide. "I knew you were wrangling cats, but you didn't say they were lions."

"I was attacked by the killer at Magnolia."

Ben set his cup on the desk. "What happened?" Greer told her story again and made sure Ben took the report. She didn't want to keep reliving the attack every time she had to tell it.

"She needs a first aid kit," Locke said.

"Oh, right. It's on Adam's desk. He had a problem with a rowdy drunk over at Shady Glen apartments during the evacuation."

"Is he okay?" Greer asked.

"I'm dandy," Adam quipped as he strode into the bullpen. Jeans. T-shirt. "And dry now."

"Where'd he get you?" His face seemed clean. No bruises.

"Everywhere." His expression was grim, but

he tossed her the first aid kit and aimed a scowl at Locke.

"She was attacked by that carny killer again," Ben offered. "I just took the report." Adam snatched it and skimmed it, then glanced at Greer, studied her face—probably the small cuts and abrasions. She was piling them up lately. "She stabbed him in the shoulder with a knitting needle."

"They're long." Greer shrugged.

Adam's eyebrows raised.

"It's all I could find."

"Well, he's wounded then. Right along with the rest of us. I guess we go up to the carnival workers and give them a good squeeze to the shoulder. Whoever flinches did it." He tossed the report on the desk and stomped out of the bullpen into the back.

This wasn't like Adam at all. She started to go after him, but Locke held her back. "Let him go, Greer."

If he didn't have a decent grasp on her arm and a strange look on his face, she would have beelined it after Adam. Confront him about not keeping her in the loop. "Fine. Let's go." Before they headed out, she also updated Ben on the box of evidence they found and the masked man who had taken it from them. Then they left the station. The rain had slackened but the skies were still full of doom and threatening another torrential storm.

"I want to talk to Rudy Dennison about Jenna's son. And I want to talk to Jenna about Bolt Masterson."

"You sure? Now?"

"I'm sure." One or all of them were hiding something. Protecting Flip. Or each other.

Locke held Lin as she slept in his arms. She'd just finished her bedtime bottle. It was almost nine. She'd stayed up as long as her little, lovely self would allow. He ought to put her down in the portable crib in Tori's room, but he couldn't make himself. Not when she was warm and snuggly against his chest, her chubby hand shoved near her lips. Her tiny breathing was rhythmic and precious. He rubbed her soft cap of hair and inhaled her baby scent.

The lamp cast a dim glow. Rain came down like white noise outside. Only rumbling thunder was loud enough to stir her—but she slept hard like her mama, who dozed on the couch, the afghan half on her legs, half on the floor. Didn't even move.

Evan and Jody were upstairs with Hollister. Tori had gone to work at the hospital.

This day had been exhausting. Locke and Greer had interviewed Rudy Dennison, who denied having an affair but admitted that Jenna's son was a drug dealer in Birmingham. He suspected he might have been supplying Tiny Tim with recreational drugs but denied he knew anything about Tiny Tim dealing. Yeah, right. Rudy also denied Flip Bomer blackmailing him.

Jenna Dennsion denied the allegations about her son as well.

Without proof the lies would never be uncovered. With no concrete leads and solid evidence, the carnival would be leaving in a few days. Locke wasn't sure where that left the killer. Would he go? Stay? Come back? He hoped after Greer injured him, he'd lay low and move on. Well, he hoped they caught him, but if he was a smart killer—and he seemed to be or he wouldn't have gotten away with so many murders for so long—he'd pack it up and go. But more victims would be left in his wake. They had to find this guy. Stop him from hurting and killing more women. Jody promised they'd stay on it. No matter what. Plus, the FBI would be in town before the carnival cleared out. Birmingham had been hit hard. Locke hadn't seen that kind of devastation in a long time. And that had only been an F3.

Now that it was quiet, with only the rainfall in the background, Locke thought back to the kiss earlier today. Right before Greer had given him an ultimatum. One he was afraid of. He'd failed so many times when he'd been given parameters to live in, work in. Rocking with his baby girl in his arms, this is where he wanted to be. Every night. But that wasn't going to happen unless he got out of the last two months of his contract and found work here. He liked Goldenville. Liked the church. The people.

Except Adam Crisp. Until he could pinpoint exactly what gave him the willies with regard to the man, he wasn't going to let Greer be alone with him. Today, Adam had been angry at Greer. Furious. When he should have been concerned.

That bothered Locke. Enough that he carefully slipped his cell phone from his pocket to text Jody just as she tiptoed into the living room. Locke raised a finger then slowly stood and put Lin to bed, flipped on her monitor, then met Jody in the kitchen. "You wanna sit out on the porch?"

"Sure." She finished pouring a glass of tea and they crept through the living room so they wouldn't disturb Greer and onto the front porch. Sitting in matching white rockers, they remained silent. Listening to the rain. Flashes of lightning illuminated the yard. "Well, what's going on?" she asked.

"Greer wants me to be in Lin's life."

"Great." She sipped her tea. "But?"

Locke leaned on his elbows. "I have to be here in Goldenville. Every day. Nine-to-five kind of work. No traveling."

Jody sat quietly. "You don't want to do that?"

"I don't know if I can, Jode. I mean…she's right. I can barely sit still for thirty minutes. How can I stay planted day in and day out?" He was torn. Conflicted. Already feeling like a selfish man and dad. "She has daddy issues and well deserved." He gave Jody the gist without revealing all the intimate details Greer had shared with him. That was private.

Jody sighed. "I see where she's coming from but Beckett travels with us and they have a baby and another one on the way. Caley is pregnant and Shepherd travels when he needs to. They come home and they're great fathers. She's afraid and not seeing that reality. Lots of parents have to travel for work. Is it the danger of your job?"

"If you haven't noticed, Greer's occupation has placed her in greater danger than mine. No, it's not that. She knows I'm careful. It's the whole idea of me leaving Lin later to do my own thing. I would never think Lin trapped me."

"But you feel caged by Greer's ultimatum."

"Yes," he murmured. "So, does that make me like her dad? Would I walk away?" Greer had him so upside down and dizzy. He was afraid he might fail his daughter. And even Greer. Definitely himself.

"Locke, you aren't Greer's dad. You can be a bit self-absorbed, sure. We all can. When it counts, you're there when you need to be. I don't have the right answer. I could tell you to suck it up and get a job here and be a dad. Or I could tell you to try to talk Greer into some sense. That you're only gone from April to end of June and you'd have some weekends in between there. That you can buy a house here and July through April you're not going anywhere. But I don't know the answer. Have you prayed?"

"Not really. I mean…not really." He laughed. "I have a hard time hearing God. I can't ever get quiet enough. My mind never settles. I'm a bad listener, too."

Jody snorted. "God knows exactly who you are, how you hear, and He can get through to you in the quiet or in the storm. He made you the way you are, Locke. Not to fail. I know you think you fail at everything you're supposed to be doing, which is why you don't settle for the 'norm,' but this baby is yours. God has a plan for you. Her. And Greer. It may be settling in like a 'normal' family or it may not. I just don't know." She stood. "I'm going to go inside and let you crack the Bible open. I know you have a Bible app on your phone."

Jody was right. "Hey, while you're inside can you have Wheezer do a deep search on Adam Crisp? He's a deputy with Greer but he's into her and today he got hurt on the job. Coincidence? Maybe. But I want to be sure."

"Sure." Jody left him on the porch, the wind sweeping a few dots of chilly rain onto his bare feet. He scrolled to his Bible app and opened it. The verse for the evening popped off the screen into his heart.

I can do all things through Christ which strengtheneth me.

All things.

His hopes of reconnecting with Greer were dashed. But there was a ton of hope where Lin was concerned. She needed him. And he needed her.

"Whatever it takes, Lord. If moving here and taking a job is the right thing and the only way to be with my daughter, then I'll do it." Isn't that what love was? Sacrifice. And God would give him strength.

He'd never been a fan of photographing people. But he could do it. Run his own studio. Do some nature photos on weekends, taking Lin with him. He could teach her the ins and outs of photography. He didn't have to be out chasing storms, helping scientists help people.

He came inside. Greer continued to snooze

on the couch. He was glad she was getting some sleep and that it wasn't restless. He kneeled beside her and brushed a strand of hair from her face. What about her? How did he feel about her? Confused. On one hand there was no escaping that he carried deep feelings for her. And not just ones from the past that had him falling in love with her in the first place, although those were still there burning bright. But in all this, the way she carried herself, the way she was an amazing mama… New feelings had developed. On the other hand, she had deceived and lied to him. Kept secrets. Locke couldn't deny being apprehensive about trusting her again… but then it was clear she didn't even want to try for a second chance, and getting back together for Lin wasn't right in his eyes. His parents had adored one another. Locke was blessed to have grown up with them as great role models. Lin deserved nothing less.

"Greer," he whispered. "Wake up. We've got to get back to your place."

She didn't stir. Exhaustion had overtaken her. Instead of forcing her awake, he stood and lingered longer than he should, battling the war going on in his heart and head.

He loved her.

That was as pure and honest as it got.

After everything. In spite of everything,

Locke loved Greer. Had always loved her even when he tried to convince himself he'd gotten over her. He never had. Never would. He wasn't here to keep her safe for Lin's sake, but for her own. Because he'd never be able to breathe again if something happened to her. He knew instantly he'd have died for his own daughter—he'd die for Greer, too.

But the heaviness in that truth smothered reality. Because he'd never be able to convince Greer that he wasn't like her dad. That he would never leave. So, he'd have to work on being content as only Lin's father.

TWELVE

Greer swiveled in her chair and toyed with a pencil at her desk at the station. She'd awoken this morning on Tori's couch. Locke on the love seat. He'd been unusually quiet and fidgety this morning even when he'd dropped her off here. She wasn't technically on duty, but she'd come in to work to at least file some papers and fill out reports. Be of some use.

"Hey."

Greer glanced up. Hollister stood with his arms over his chest.

"What are you doing here? I thought you were going to finish cleaning out the storage unit and attic this morning."

"I got most of it done, but I got a call. My pastor's little girl—she's four—went missing. They had eyes on her one minute while at the park this morning and then the next minute she'd vanished." Hollister's voice was strained and his eyes held a mix of concern and fear. "Just…gone."

Greer stood and embraced her big, burly brother with the softest heart known to man. "I'm so sorry. I wish I could come and help with the search. I'll keep the girl and your pastor's family in my prayers."

"Grace is leading the charge. She called me an hour ago when it was clear she wasn't going to be found by her parents."

Grace Thackery had been in Hollis's life for the past two years, since he'd found her left for dead and with no memory on the banks of the Mississippi River. She now volunteered with the search-and-rescue team. "How is Grace? Any news on her situation?"

"The private eye she hired has hit nothing but dead ends." He shrugged.

"I hope she finds some answers about her past soon."

Hollis nodded. "Me too. But if anyone can find Pastor Reed's baby girl, it's Grace. It's like she was born for this kind of work."

"Maybe she was."

"Maybe." He flicked a pen on her desk. "I don't want to leave but I know you're safe, and Jody and Evan are a blink away…and then there's Locke."

Greer sighed and sunk into the office chair. "He wants to be part of Lin's life, Hollister."

Hollister rubbed his scruffy chin. "And? You don't want that?"

"I can't knowingly allow him to love and then leave our daughter. She'll live with that guilt her whole life and—"

"Back the bus up," Hollister said with a measure of sternness in his voice as he kneeled in front of her. "Why would she live with guilt? If Locke decides to walk out—which I don't think he would—how is that her responsibility? Why should it fall on her shoulders?" He cocked his head and squinted, studying her. "Greer, tell me you haven't been blaming yourself for what our jerk of a dad did?"

Greer's bottom lip quivered. "I heard him that night, Hollis. He said we trapped him. Mama getting pregnant was her way of keeping him tied down and he wanted out. We did that."

"No, ma'am, we did not. He was selfish and made a choice. I know it hurt. I hurt. But at some point, you have to let God heal you so you can be free of that. And free to trust another person. To trust Locke."

"I'm scared," she admitted. "And I don't know how to let God heal me. I don't even know how to start. Not really. This pain, this guilt and overwhelming fear, it's—it's become part of me." She'd carried it since she was a child. If she hadn't come home to Mama when she was sick, part of her might have found a way to sabotage her relationship with Locke later on down the road. To back out before he abandoned her. "He's so much like Dad."

"And I see so many things about him that aren't. Locke isn't selfish and the choices he's made, to stick around and risk his life for Lin and for you—there's no resentment in him. It's not a chore to protect you and his daughter. Just coming to my baseball game was a chore for Dad when he wanted to be out with his buddies at the bar. He missed birthdays because he'd scheduled fishing trips. All. Selfish."

Hollis was right. Dad missed a million events and big things to be off doing his own thing. "Locke chases storms. One adventure after another."

"And he gets paid for it. It's called a job. That's not selfish." Hollister lightly clipped her chin. "Dad didn't give up anything to settle down and be a father because he never settled down. He used us as an excuse to freeload off our mother half the time and have his cake and eat it, too. I think at one time he loved Mama but he loved himself more. I don't see that in Locke. And if you can get past the fear and really look, I don't think you'll see that, either."

Greer's heart was about to burst. Hollister's words warred with what Greer had believed for so long. She threw herself into his arms and buried her head in his neck. "What would I do without a brother like you?"

"Never get that attic and garage cleaned out for one." He pressed a kiss on the top of her head. "I love you. I want you to be happy, Greer. Happy and whole, okay?"

Greer wanted that, too.

"What about you? Are you happy?" He may have healed and held no resentment or guilt over Dad's abandonment, but his eyes never fully lit up. He'd never married, either. If it wasn't over fear of being abandoned then why was he still alone?

"I'm doing fine, baby sister. Don't you worry about me." His words held no confidence. But she knew not to press. If Hollister didn't want to talk, he wouldn't. No amount of pestering or even torture would break him. He was iron inside and out. "I'll be back as soon as we find Lilly Reed, okay?"

"I'm going to be fine, too. Focus on that little girl, not me." She patted his scruffy cheek. "Call me when you find her."

"I will." He tousled her hair. "Greer, one thing that helped me was knowing that no matter who leaves me, God promised He never would. He never leaves us. Abandons us. And at the end of the day, His love is greater and stronger. I can survive anything knowing that nothing separates me from God's love. That's how I made it through two tours, and it's how I made it through knowing that our dad didn't care enough about me to stick around."

God had promised that, but Greer hadn't focused on it. Hadn't let that truth soothe her wounded heart like salve. Instead, she'd focused on the one man who had broken his promise. And feared all other men might, too.

What would happen if she found peace in knowing no matter what… God loved her unconditionally and would never abandon her? Even with a killer after her, He was with her. He'd surrounded her with people who cared about her and loved her. People had flown in to help her out. She worked three jobs, but she had the jobs. Ends barely met…but they met. She was lonely often…but then how many times did she let the loneliness consume her instead of turning the pages of scripture and letting God's love, grace and mercy consume her?

Hollis squeezed her shoulder and left her spinning in the chair and rolling his words around in her heart.

After a few hours of paperwork, Ben Garrison swung by with a couple of chocolate croissants and a to-go cup of coffee from the bakery across the street. Smart idea putting pastries and coffee across from the sheriff's station. "You look like the weight of the world is on your shoulders," Ben said.

"Well, I do have a serial killer trying to take me down, so there's that." She bit into the flaky, buttery crust and a burst of rich, dark chocolate exploded on her tongue. She chased it down with a nutty, bitter brew. Perfection. "I haven't seen Adam since yesterday." When he'd seemed so angry at her.

"He took a sick day."

That probably explained his crankiness. He'd been coming down with something, or the beat down by the drunk could have attributed.

Greer's phone rang. She glanced at the screen. Cindy Woolridge. "Hey, Cin, what's up?"

"How are you? Everything okay?"

"For now. I'm at the station working, unofficially." Thanks to the serial killer.

"I need a favor if you have time."

"Okay."

"Mark Whittle came down with the flu—it's going around—and he's supposed to get some soccer team shots this afternoon—"

"It's supposed to storm this afternoon. You know that, right? And won't the fields be muddy?" Greer asked.

"Yes to all of that, but I'll be honest. I'm being selfish. Michael has to be out of town for the first two weeks in May, and I don't want him to miss the picture with the boys. Next year they won't be on the same team since Jeff will move up in the age division and Michael will only be their coach this once. Storms aren't set to come in until after five. I've been monitoring. Pictures are at three thirty."

"All right. I can do it." The boys would grow up and have that memory with their father. Being together. Playing together. Photos of Greer and her dad were few and far between. She couldn't judge Cindy for this. She checked the time. One hour. "I owe you for so much."

"Offer is still open if you need help with Lin."

"I appreciate that."

"I'll see you there. Kids have practice after the photo shoot—if the weather holds—and I'm the snack mama."

Greer didn't know how Cindy did it all. They'd no doubt be homemade snacks. "Save me a treat," Greer said, then ended the call and grabbed her things. "I'm heading out to the soccer field. Team photos and practice. If you need me, call. I'm taking a deputy's vehicle. Sheriff won't mind."

Ben indulged in his second croissant. "You want company?"

"Company or a babysitter?"

A sheepish grin creased Ben's baby-faced cheeks. "Tomato, to-mah-to."

She retrieved her gun from the desk drawer, holstered it and grabbed the bag with the last croissant from Ben. "Thanks."

Outside, chills broke out across her arms and neck. She searched the lot and saw no one.

But something ominous seemed to ride the wind, prickling her skin. Watching. Waiting.

Locke whistled to grab Greer's attention and she jumped three feet in the air. "You scared me half to death," she said, clutching her heart. "Were you watching me?"

"No. I just pulled up. Where are you going all by yourself? You know it's not safe, right?"

Greer sighed. "I was going to text you when I got inside the car. I have a photo shoot in an hour at the soccer fields. I need to set up."

Locke checked his time. "Storms are coming. Bad ones."

"Not until after. I'll be done quick."

Locke rubbed the back of his neck. He'd been with the team all day, researching and tracking storm systems. He'd been editing and tagging photos for hours, but the last hour and a half he'd done something else. "Do you have time for me to show you something? Then I'll drop you off at the fields unless you need the deputy vehicle. You can follow."

"I can ride with you. Cindy can bring me back. Where are we going?" She followed him to his truck and climbed inside.

"Somewhere." He half grinned but his stomach was in knots. After talking to Jody and trying super hard to be still and quiet with hopes of knowing where and how God was leading him, he made a decision. Wasn't sure it was the right one or what Greer would think, but he had to prove somehow that he was a worthy dad who would never skip out on his kid.

He'd also visited the bank before coming by. Now he made a right on Main Street and drove past a cluster of houses that led to the far side of town, only ten minutes from Greer's place. He pulled into the small driveway of the farmhouse. Rolling pastures behind. Horses. Three bedrooms.

"What is going on?" Greer asked.

Locke swallowed the lump in his throat. "You said you wanted me to settle down. To move here. To be a full-time dad. Be home every night. This morning I saw this house for rent. I called. It's affordable. And the horses can be ridden if

I'll do the feeding and muck the stalls. Lin might like riding horses, don't you think?"

Greer sat as still as a statue, staring straight ahead. "You want to rent a farmhouse and live here?"

Open land. Great places for nature pictures or even family portraits. "I want to be in our daughter's life, Greer. And I'm willing to do whatever it takes to prove it. If that means I need to join the force and do some side photography, then that's what I'll do. Because love is about sacrifice." He stared Greer straight in the eye. "I love Lin."

"Sacrifice," she whispered and tears welled in her eyes. "Opposite of selfishness." Greer didn't seem to be addressing him, just talking in general. He sat quietly.

"I could put a tree swing right here in front. She'd like that." This wasn't ideal but the more he resolved in his heart to make the changes necessary to be with his daughter, the more excited he became. Until he thought of seeing Greer every day. She may never trust Locke—would always be waiting for the shoe to drop and him to leave. She'd keep herself guarded from him, but she might be open to love someone else. That thought turned his gut and soured his mood. It would be excruciating to watch Greer fall in love with another man.

But this wasn't about Greer. It was about their daughter.

"I don't know what to say," Greer murmured.

The other thing Locke wanted was to give Greer what she was owed financially. He opened the glove box and pulled out an envelope. "We've discussed this, too, but fair is fair, Greer. You shouldn't have had to provide for Lin alone all these months, plus the prenatal care. So I moved some money around this morning and I want you to have this." He handed her the envelope.

Slowly, she opened it and gasped. "Locke… this is a lot of money. I can't—"

"You can. You should. It's only right." He didn't have many expenses and while he was impulsive, he wasn't much of an impulsive spender. He'd saved most of his money. No one deserved it more than Greer and Lin. "I don't want it back but if you refuse, I'll put it in a savings account for her college fund or something. But, I'd rather you take it now and lighten some of your load."

Greer pressed the heels of her hands to her eyes, her lips quivering. She gave a quick nod of acceptance and inhaled deeply. "I need to get to the soccer field."

Okay. So much for conversation, but it was a start. She hadn't refused the money and she hadn't protested him renting this house. He still had to talk to the research team leader. He may have to finish out his two months, but surely Greer would see his planning as a step in the right direction. And if he could follow through with his work commitment, maybe she'd believe he'd follow through with his parental commitment.

He backed out of the driveway.

"Did you sign the lease?"

He had. Even if he had to finish up his two months, he'd pay the rent to keep the place for when he could move in. "I did."

Greer didn't say much more than that. Thunderheads rolled in but a few sprays of sunshine popped through the clouds as he pulled into the soccer-field complex. Cars littered the parking lot. Kids ran around as if storms weren't coming in. Parents chatted with one another. "Bad day for photos," Locke noted.

"Yeah. Is what it is. I'll be about an hour."

Locke clicked his back teeth together. "I have to work, Greer. I was hoping you'd be safe at the precinct all day." That he would prefer.

"Look around, it's chock-full of people. It's not like a sparse park. And I'm steering clear of Porta Potties these days."

"Har. Har." He didn't love the idea, but she was right. She hopped from the truck and tossed him a half smile. A war was going on in her eyes, but now wasn't the time to ask questions. He'd let her process it all. A gust of wind whipped her hair. "I got a bad feeling, Greer. If it suddenly quiets down or you see any rotation near the rain base…get Cindy and get out. Okay?"

"I will." She clutched her camera to her chest and closed the door, jogging toward the fields.

Locke waited a beat then headed back to the mobile unit, about six miles south, where all the action was predicted to take place. He'd never dreaded bad weather more in all his life.

THIRTEEN

Greer weaved and bobbed through the crowds of parents watching practice. She waved to several people she knew, spotting Cindy by Complex C. She rushed over and hugged her.

Cindy grinned. "I so owe you for this."

"No way. We're even."

Michael jogged up in his white-and-purple coach's jersey. "Let her owe you with a pie. She'll make two and I'll have dessert for a few nights." He winked and kissed Cindy's cheek. "But seriously, thanks for this. I got called out on an emergency construction job. Bad stuff in Birmingham. They need help with rebuilding."

Greer had watched that on the news the other night. Businesses and residential districts had been wrecked. "At least it'll only be for two weeks."

"For now." He waved at the assistant coach and glanced at the sky. "I hope you have time to do the photos."

"Round everyone up. I'll get started." She turned to Cindy. "How many teams am I photographing?"

"Four."

Could be worse. Thunder lightly rumbled in the distance. "Let's get moving then."

Greer waited while Michael corralled his team of rowdy soccer players. Her skin crawled and she scanned the area as a tremor of fear awakened in her bones. A hand clamped on her shoulder and she flinched, shrieked.

"Hey. It's just me."

Greer spun and Adam stood there, a grin on his face.

"You scared me."

"I noticed. Ben said you were here. I don't see Lin's father." He glanced around.

"He's working. What's up?" Adam wore his deputy's uniform, unlike her. "I thought you were taking a sick day."

"I was. Got called in."

In the last twenty minutes? "For what?"

"Standby for storms." He waved off the conversation. "I want to talk to you about something. Can we go somewhere?"

"I can't right now. I'm about to shoot some soccer-team photos."

"Lot of ears here. Can I wait for you?"

Better they have a private conversation. She couldn't be sure what Adam wanted to say, but she knew what she wanted to. Locke may have been right. Adam had turned moody when Locke had arrived in town, and with all the time he was spending with Greer… If this was about having feelings for her, then she needed a place to let him down easy. "Yeah. I shouldn't be too long. How are you feeling? I know you were beat up yesterday."

Adam winced. "Sore but making it."

"Same." She gave him a friendly smile, as sisterly as possible. Wind picked up as thunderheads built. Then suddenly the wind died. The air didn't even stir. "This ain't good."

People paused, gazed at the sky and murmured about the weather. A few parents wrangled their children and sprinted across the wide-open field. Greer needed to move fast. "Cin!" she called and touched Adam's arm. "I have to go."

She raced to Cindy. "I may only be able to get y'all's soccer team done before the weather gets brutal. It's looking ugly."

"It seems pretty calm to me. I can see the sun."

Meant nothing. "Let's get moving."

The same creepy feeling slithered over her skin, pulling and tugging at her.

"Doppler is showing signs of severe weather moving in and rapidly," Jerry said. "Locke, can you head northeast and get video and photos as it moves in?"

"Roger that." Locke signed off and hung a hard right on the back road leading outside of Goldenville. The conditions were ripe for a supercell storm and that meant possible tornado. Already a warning had been placed in the surrounding counties.

Greenish sky. Quiet atmosphere. Locke didn't like it. His phone rang and he pressed the Bluetooth speaker on his steering wheel. "Hey, Jode, everything okay? Lin isn't sick or hurt, is she?"

"No, nothing like that," Jody said. "We are watching the weather, though. News just broke in to regular programming and Evan has on his satellite radio. You in the thick of it?"

"I have a feeling I'm about to be. 'Bout to get some footage. What's up?" He pulled to the side of the road and hopped out, switching to his earpiece. He grabbed his camera and strode down the ditch into the plowed-up field that reached for miles in both directions. Clouds overheard grew sooty, more ominous. He took advantage and went to work getting the necessary shots.

"Wheezer called me."

If the computer analyst at her security company was calling then there was news. "What did he find?"

"Well, the crummy news is he couldn't find

one employee who worked all the carnivals during the time of the murders."

"It's possible someone kept shoddy records." He gauged the wind. It had picked up again, gaining momentum and blowing his hair in every direction and his denim jacket open.

"Right, but that's not the case here. Wheezer hunted for missing persons reports using the same traits as the victims. Brunettes with blue eyes. He broadened the age range from eighteen to twenty-nine. We got a hit."

"Okay," Locke said and studied the weather. Took a few more photos and some footage.

"A nineteen-year-old girl went missing from a carnival called the Dixie Entertainment twelve years ago in Decatur. She worked as a knife-throwing assistant."

Locke fumbled with the camera. "Did they find her?"

"No. So we can't determine the way she died or even if she's dead. But everything else fits. And… Flip Bomer worked the carnival at that time. He was twenty-five."

Locke raked his hands through his hair, every nerve in his body on fire. "The blackmailing has to do with a missing girl—likely murdered by the guy who killed Flip, Tiny Tim and attacked Greer—doesn't it?"

"It's possible. If Flip is the blackmailer everyone says he is, he could have been blackmailing the killer and he'd had enough after all this time and offed him."

But why now? Why after twelve years? Could Flip have only recently discovered the killer's crime? Or recently blackmailed him?

"Locke, only one other man was on payroll who fits the bill—that we know of, due to such poor employment records—at the Dixie Entertainment carnival during that time."

"Who?"

Greer used an elastic cloth hair band to pull her unruly mop into a ponytail. The wind was cutting up and sunlight was slowly disappearing. The eight-and nine-year-old boys weren't cooperating. Three were wrestling in the mud, two more were running around the goal.

Michael clapped his hands. "Okay, team. I mean it now. Huddle up."

A dot of rain pecked Greer's arm. This photo may not get done at all.

"Greer! We're ready," Michael called. She blinked as a few more pops of rain dotted her cheeks.

She held up the camera and zoomed in. "Scooch in, y'all!"

"Pile up!" Jeff, Michael's oldest, hooted and went full-on linebacker toward his dad.

Greer lowered her camera as Jeff and Greg, along with two other yahoos, dove onto Michael. She used the opportunity to capture the shot as Michael groaned and winced as they dog-piled him. She took several more. "Okay for real now." Out of the corner of her eye, she noticed Adam was gone from the first row of bleachers. Guess he didn't want to wait.

"Get it together, boys," the assistant coach boomed and the boys fell into line.

Greer positioned the camera and zoomed in. Her lungs morphed into iron and her breath caught. She zoomed in again. Her hand trembled.

She eased the camera down.

Nothing.

Picked the camera back up, went into zoom position and saw it again.

Minute. Just a drop of blood leaching through the shirt on his shoulder.

As she lowered the camera again, Michael met her gaze. Greer stumbled backward. It was there for the first time since she'd met him a year and a half ago. The facade had faltered, like a curtain being pulled back, revealing his truest form.

Evil.

And for the first time, Greer recognized his eyes. The same eyes of the killer. She couldn't make herself look away. Hate. Murder. A glint of sick amusement dancing in them.

This man had…he'd kept her own child in his home! She'd placed her trust in him. Sat with him at lunch and even church, and thanked him for taking care of Lin. A new wave of nausea flooded her. Why? Why did Michael Woolridge murder Flip Bomer? And so many other women?

Cindy! The woman was clueless. She doted on Michael, who traveled for his work at times, giving him prime opportunity to track carnivals and hunt victims. He was leaving for two weeks in Birmingham to help rebuild, but was that one-hundred-percent true? Had he zeroed in on another carnival in the area?

Instantly, lightning struck and the winds turned violent, blowing over chairs, purses, goals and coolers. But Michael's eyes remained on hers, daring her to make a move.

In the distance, tornado sirens wailed.

"Go!"

"Run!"

People screamed and scooped up children, racing from the field to the safety of their cars. But Greer stood firm. Michael's blood spot grew larger—the boys had reinjured where Greer had stabbed him with the knitting needle.

He'd tried to kill her. Multiple times. He knew where she lived and broke in so she wouldn't suspect him. Cindy had a key. His job had him on-site in many locations. It would be easy to follow Greer, find out where she was and take the opportunities to strike. He must have told Cindy work had come up Saturday night and left only to attack Greer. And was at church singing on Sunday morning!

The wind pressed against Greer—she dug her heels into the ground to stay upright.

Kids cried and wailed.

Men shielded women and worked to guide them to the parking lot as the tornado sirens screeched.

"Michael," Cindy screamed through the wild winds. "We have to get the kids out of here! Alert says a tornado touched down less than ten miles out!"

Michael's eyes lingered on Greer. "Get the boys. Get to safety. I'm going to help out here."

"But Michael!" she cried.

He leaned over and, while staring at Greer, kissed his wife's cheek. Greer's stomach roiled. "Get to safety," he boomed. "Be careful. I love you."

Love? Love was his cover. To hide the vile creature that lived inside him. Masqueraded as a family man. A churchgoer. A father. A leader in the community. Greer's skin crawled.

Cindy grabbed the boys and slowed near Greer. "Come on, Greer."

"I'm going to help out here first." She mimicked Michael's own words. He was helping no one but himself.

It was over. He knew she knew. There were two choices. Try to take out Greer without anyone noticing. Nope. She had a gun. She placed her hand on it. Patted it. The second choice would be for him to make a run for it. And she would be on him like green on grass.

He glanced at her gun and grinned. He wasn't afraid. Not of her.

Greer couldn't deny that she was afraid of him.

In a whirl of mayhem, the soccer field cleared. Trees cracked and popped in the distance. Michael glanced in their direction. Through a wooded bike path was a subdivision.

He was going to run. Disappear. His cover here was blown.

But Greer and Lin would never be safe.

Other women would never be safe. A killer didn't stop killing.

Not until he was caught.

Michael bolted toward the trees.

Greer had no choice. She gave chase.

Locke pressed on the gas pedal and drove at breakneck speed toward the soccer complex. Michael Woolridge used to go by the name Mick Woolridge. Grew up with a drunk for a father and traveled with Dixie Entertainment starting at the age of ten. He was mentored and trained in knife impalement until he'd gotten his own show. Mindy Bridges had been his assistant. When she went missing, no one had suspected Michael—a courteous young man of twenty-eight. He'd had a solid alibi. Flip Bomer. He'd continued his travels with Dixie Entertainment for about six months more and then stuck around in Birmingham working construction. When the tornadoes came through Goldenville almost twelve years ago, Michael had been on the crew. Met Cindy. Married her in a hurry.

A disguise to keep killing? How hard would it have been to check websites and map out traveling carnivals, then lie about construction work taking him out of town? Not hard at all. Seemed, according to Wheezer and Jody, that's exactly what he'd done. Right here under their noses. Locke had eaten with the man. Allowed his daughter to spend the night with him. What if he'd hurt her? His head spun and bile rose in his throat as he yanked the wheel to the left, avoiding a wheelbarrow lying in the middle of the road.

Jerry and his team had spotted the tornado. Locke hadn't been close enough, but it was heading this way. And Greer was at the fields with her attacker. And no vehicle! He'd tried calling but had gotten voicemail.

As oncoming traffic headed for him, exiting the soccer field, he pressed down on the gas pedal and squealed into the lot. He jumped from his truck. Most everyone was gone but he grabbed the shoulder of a man who was with his wife and older kid. "Do you know Greer Montgomery?" Locke bellowed over the wind and thunder.

"Yeah. She's down on the field. Or she...was. You better get out of here and to safety." He urged the woman on and they raced to the red truck in the lot. Pushing against the gales, Locke sprinted to the edge of the soccer fields. In the distance, Greer was running into the woods.

Was she crazy?

His lungs squeezed and blood whooshed in his head. He heard it first.

A roar announcing its arrival. Its intent.

He whipped his head to the left.

The twister was eating up the ground, heading straight for Greer. The woods would be nothing but her death warrant.

Locke couldn't stand by and do nothing.

Not when the woman he loved was running into death's door.

Praying under his breath, Locke kicked up dust and raced with the cyclone into the woods, knowing it was absolutely futile but needing to press on, press in. Trees uprooted in its path; the roof of the concession complex blew over Locke's head, sending his heart into his throat, but he charged toward the woods. Too much debris and wind in his eyes to see.

No one was coming out of this alive.

FOURTEEN

Greer's breath left her lungs as the terrorizing roar deafened her ears. The tornado was heading right into the woods. Trees were uprooting and being tossed like toothpicks. Greer could hardly see. Couldn't think. The wind was too strong. Rain descended, stinging her skin.

She pushed forward. Michael couldn't get away, but Greer couldn't see him!

From nowhere, he grabbed her and slammed her to the ground. He raised his knife.

"How could you?" she shouted. "Why?" She shrieked as the sounds of wood splitting like twigs came closer. They were going to die. Lin was going to be motherless. But Locke. She had Locke and he would be a good dad. In her heart, she knew it. He'd rented a house and was willing to sacrifice the life he'd always dreamed of having to settle down.

The way he talked about riding horses and swings. The way he'd kissed her.

He wouldn't leave Lin. And her daughter had Tori, Jody and Hollister as well.

"Flip! He was going to ruin everything. Coming into town and seeing all I've built here and wanting a piece of the pie. He thought he could blackmail me about Mindy."

Who was Mindy? She fought to free herself from the ground, but he was too strong. The winds were too strong.

"I should have killed him after he lied for me all those year ago when I killed her, but I didn't. My mistake. I'd never taken a life before." He leaned into her face, down into her ear. "But I liked it."

Greer kneed him in the stomach and went for the knife.

"What about Tiny Tim?" She clutched his wrist, hoping to knock the weapon away.

"Recognized me talking to Flip earlier that day. I couldn't have witnesses identifying me and placing me with him. He had to die. And so do you."

Michael had children. A wife. He was just going to kill her and hope to flee? To slide into a new life and identity and keep killing? Or go back to being the upstanding citizen. They had no leads!

He raised the knife as a chilling crack came. Suddenly, a tree slammed into Michael, thrusting him like a rag doll into the air and impaling him against another tree. Greer gaped, stunned. Her brain said to run. Her body remained paralyzed.

Another sound pierced the terrifying drone of the twister making its way to her. She squinted. She didn't have long.

A blur to her right sprung closer.

No. No. No.

He was supposed to be safe. He was supposed to give their daughter a life. A parent.

Not be here with her. Not die alongside her. Everything inside her sank. Lin was about to be an orphan. Greer had been so scared Locke would be a dad who left—she never thought it would be from trying to save Greer.

He grabbed her hand. "Run! Run, Greer!" He glanced at a dead Michael Woolridge impaled on a tree like a target on the death wheel. Locke yanked her along as they worked to beat the tornado barreling down on them, but Greer wasn't stupid and neither was Locke.

They weren't making it out of this. People didn't outrun twisters.

Bits of bark and twigs bit into her skin. Pine needles pricked her like daggers.

Locke held tight, dragging her with him. Her feet came out from under her and she fell to the ground. "Go! Go on. I—I can't make it, Locke.

Get out of here and don't let our daughter be an orphan. Please!"

Yanking her to her feet, Locke glanced behind her. "You will not die today, Greer Montgomery. Where's the feisty, brave woman I know?"

Exhausted. Defeated. Aching in pain. Waterlogged from the torrential rain.

"Lin needs her mother."

A wave of bravery rose within her. Lin. Lin needed her. She found renewed strength, even if the situation was hopeless. There was no escape from the man-eater coming for them. Up ahead she spotted a steep ditch with a waterdrainage tunnel. On the other side was a small subdivision.

"It's our only hope!" Locke roared.

The twister ate through the trees, blowing Locke and her off balance before they could make a leap. They rolled down the ditch and Locke scurried to shove Greer in first. "Go! I'm right behind you."

Greer scrambled through the freezing waters into the tunnel.

Locke came in behind.

The sound of death boomed and churned. Roofs screamed in protest as they ripped from houses and glass shattered. Greer prayed those inside their homes were safe.

A surge of water flooded the tunnel, racing over her face as the twister destroyed everything above them. "Locke!" she shrieked.

"Hold on. Just hold on, baby!"

The waters rose inside.

The tornado raged outside.

Either way they were dead.

The waters rose to her chin.

She gulped in air as it covered her nose…her head. Nowhere to find air. No way to leave. Not with the whirlwind wreaking havoc.

Locke's hand laced with hers and squeezed. In that connection, somehow, she felt his love. He'd come for her. And he'd stayed with her. He was going to die because of her. This wasn't selfish. He was not like her dad. Hollister was right.

God, forgive me. It wasn't too late for that.

Her lungs burned and her brain screamed for oxygen. But it was too late to tell Locke how she felt. That she loved him. Had always loved him.

Her body wrenched in pain as she fought to hold on.

Locke's fingers squeezed hers again as if trying to buoy her faith, remind her that she wasn't alone. They could make it.

Maybe they could.

Until she saw nothing. Heard nothing.

Felt nothing.

* * *

Greer's hand went limp and panic surged through Locke's veins as he held on and held out for life. Come on. *God, help us. Help us. Please!*

The cyclone whirred above them. His lungs burned and begged for air. He wasn't sure how much longer he had, and with Greer's relaxed grip, he was terrified. He couldn't raise their daughter alone. *God, I can't do this alone. I need You.*

Suddenly, the roaring disappeared and he swam through the tunnel, pulling Greer along with him until he reached the opening and pulled them onto dry land. Greer's face was bleached, her lips blue.

She didn't move. He straddled her and shoved a clump of hair from the side of her face, felt for a pulse.

His hands trembled and the backs of his eyes burned like glowing coals.

There was no pulse. He turned her head to the side as water spilled from her mouth, then centered her, opened her airway and gave her two rescue breaths.

He cried out until his lungs ached and placed his hands on her chest as he began compressions. Tears fell down his cheeks and his nose ran, but he counted them off and pled and begged God to save her.

What would he tell Lin? Nothing. Because Greer was going to live.

One and...two and...

"Please, Greer! Live, baby. Live! Don't leave me."

Five and...six and...

"I can't do this without you. I don't want to. I love you."

Nine and...ten and...

He continued to do compressions. Finished the first cycle. Started the second.

This could not be happening.

A gurgling came from her mouth. He hurried and turned her to her side, relief flooding him faster than the waters in the drainage tunnel. She coughed and sputtered and threw up a heap of water.

"Greer! Oh, thank you. Greer!"

She continued coughing and gagging, then sat up. She gazed at Locke, then fell into his arms, sobbing. He stroked her matted wet hair. "It's okay. You're okay now. We're—we're okay now."

Cradling her, he rocked her back and forth, never wanting to let go, but a new wave of hysteria hit him. "Lin! Jody. We need a phone."

Locke helped Greer to her wobbly feet and supported her weight as they climbed from the ditch to the road. Houses were rubble. People wandered dazed in the streets. Wails and moans of mothers and fathers echoed in the distance. This kind of destruction had to have been an F4.

They found a man sitting with his family, staring into space. "Sir, can we use your phone?"

He absently handed them his cell phone and Greer made the call. "Tori! Are you safe?" She nodded at Locke. "They went into the root cellar."

Locke heaved a sigh.

Greer returned the phone to the man and went into cop mode, aiding the injured. Locke fell into line, helping pull loved ones and pets from the debris.

Neighbors hugged one another. Cried with one another. Prayed with one another.

Fatalities had been racked up and Locke grieved the devastation, but he couldn't help but be thankful that Greer was alive. Lin and his sister and brother-in-law were safe.

Sirens whirred and Deputies Garrison and Crisp arrived on the scene with firetrucks and ambulances. Adam ran for Greer and hugged her. "Are you okay?"

"I am now," she said. "Locke saved me."

Adam put distance between him and Greer and nodded at Locke. "Good. I'm glad you were here." Sincerity shone in his eyes. He touched Greer's cheek. "We'll talk later."

"What happened to you? At the soccer field."

"Tornado hit the edge of town before it disappeared and landed here. I got called out."

Greer tucked a strand of hair behind her ear. "Okay."

She didn't mention they'd find Michael Woolridge in the woods. Or what had happened. She let them get to their jobs. But she turned to Locke. "I can't tell Cindy who her husband really was. I don't want those boys growing up knowing their father was a monster."

"You want them to believe he died in the tornado a hero or something?" Locke wasn't sure that was the right thing to do even though he understood where Greer was coming from.

"I do. But those victims' families deserve closure, and I know as heartbroken and devastated as Cindy will be, she'd want that. How did you know?"

"Jody called." He explained the connection and listened as Greer retold Michael's admissions. Greer used Adam's radio and called the sheriff, delivering the news as he arrived. She wanted to tell Cindy about Michael, but Sheriff Wright insisted he be the one to inform her.

Hours later, Greer and Locke trudged onto Tori's porch. Locke's bones were weary and his muscles ached. But when he saw Lin and she reached for him, everything relaxed. The pain seemed to disappear. He took his baby girl and peppered her with hugs and kisses, then he passed her to Greer, who smothered her with more. He hugged Jody and Evan and quietly told them what happened while Greer loved on their daughter.

He caught her eye and Greer smiled. But it wasn't the smile that undid him. It was what was in her eyes. Something he thought he'd glimpsed on the carousel at first. Something he had definitely seen when they dated.

He saw love.

And hope.

"How about I take Lin inside and change her?" Tori asked.

"I need to call Wilder and give him an update," Jody said.

"I need to…go with her," Evan said.

They left them to some privacy on the porch. Locke closed the distance between them and cradled Greer's face. "I thought I'd lost you."

"I thought I'd been lost. Locke—"

"Me first." He grinned. This woman. She was everything to him. "I love you. And I don't know what it will take to prove that I'm not going anywhere. I'm never leaving you or Lin. I don't care how long it takes. You're not just the mother of my child. You're the love of my life." He searched her eyes, tears blurring his. "When you weren't breathing… I wasn't breathing. Because I can't—I can't breathe without you, Greer. Please give me a chance. Just one."

A strangled sob croaked from Greer and she sniffed, laying her forehead on his. "I'm so sorry for everything. I was so afraid and my fear kept me from telling you the truth. Not just about Lin…but the truth about me. I was scared of getting hurt again. Locklin, I never stopped loving you. I've never loved anyone else. It may take me some time, but I'm going to work through my fear. I may even need counseling, but I want to get past this. And I want you to forgive me."

He kissed her brow. "I forgive you," he whispered. "And I'll be here. I'll do whatever you need."

"And please don't quit your job." She peered into his eyes. "You love it and you're not gone forever. You have weekends sometimes. We can come and see you until Lin starts school. We can make it work. I was wrong to put demands on you. I wanted to constrict you to prove you'd walk away…but I don't really want you to give up your work. Not to make you stay but because I want that for you."

She wanted him to keep his job. To renew the contract? His heart nearly burst. He had no more words, only action. He slipped his hand around her neck and gently descended on her lips, claiming them for himself, as his own. She tasted like goodness. Like love. Like freedom.

EPILOGUE

A week had passed since the tornado's destruction. Cindy was devastated and she and Greer had cried together. Jody and Evan had flown back to Atlanta. Lin was staying in her own bed and the town was rebuilding the south end.

Adam had found the box of evidence stolen from Greer and Locke that night in Flip's camper. Bolt Masterson had taken it to help Jenna. He was going to do some jail time.

They'd searched the Woolridges' home and found a false back in Michael's closet along with trinkets he'd kept over the years from his victims. The prosthetic nose, the beard and mustache had been in a bag with knives along with the trophies he'd kept to relive his murders. There were more than seven. FBI were working on the case and notifying families. The carnival had packed up and left, taking their secrets with them. Greer had called the Birmingham police about Jenna Dennison's son being a drug dealer.

Adam had come by yesterday while Locke was finishing up his work with the research team. He'd admitted his feelings for Greer and that he had come to the soccer field to see if there was a chance for them. But after seeing her and Locke in the aftermath of the tornado, he knew there wasn't one and he was dealing with that. He'd wished her and Locke the best.

Hollister had called. Grace had found Lilly Reed and she was now back in the arms of her parents, safe and sound.

Greer sat on a blanket with Lin in the front yard and watched her stack colorful rings onto a plastic white stick.

Locke pulled into the drive and bounded from the truck, sending her pulse rocketing. "How're my best girls?" he asked and collapsed on the blanket beside them.

"We're good. How did it go with the team?"

"They got a lot of good data and it looks like they're getting another two-year grant. But I declined."

"What?" She thought he was going to keep doing what he loved.

Locke's crooked smile sent her pulse skittering. "I'm going to finish out this contract. Which means some traveling in tornado alley, but I can be home on some weekends and you two can come see me. You know I'll make sure you're safe."

"I know. We'll figure it out. Make it work. But what about after the two months?"

Locke skimmed her jawline with his thumb. "I called Rush and Nora."

Why would he call her cousin Rush and his wife in Tennessee? Unless… Nora worked as a private meteorologist and storm tracker. "Are you moving us to Splendor Pines?" she teased.

"No, but I do the like the mountains. I asked her to put out some feelers here locally. Channel Six is looking for someone with experience in storm chasing. The job's mine if I want it. And I plan to still sell nature photos and help you build this photography-studio business. Memories are priceless. I want us to help others make them."

Greer was stunned speechless.

Locke's smile turned mischievous. "One thing. The name has to change. Greer Montgomery Photography won't do."

Greer rolled her eyes. "Yeah? What are you changing it to?"

"Well… Montgomery-Gallagher Studios had a nice ring to it, but then I realized that wouldn't work, either." He leaned in and nuzzled her nose.

"Why not?" Her stomach dipped.

"Because, you're not always going to be a

Montgomery." He pecked her nose and shifted to his knee, removing a velvet box from his pocket. "Greer Montgomery, I bought this ring two years ago and I wasn't able to give it to you then, but I couldn't let it go because I could never let you go. Will you do me the honor of being my wife?"

Greer's heart soared. "Yes, I will."

Lock placed the oval diamond ring on her finger and drew her into his safe arms—arms that promised to always hold her, to protect her. He kissed her wilder than a whirlwind and she melded against him. God had blessed her with this second chance. She'd been open to healing, to trusting again, and the peace and joy gushed like a river.

She drew away. "So, what are we calling our business?"

"I was thinking Fidgety Photos. Tagline— we'll capture the shot anyway." He laughed. "No? LLG Studios then?"

LLG Studios. Locklin, Lin and Greer. A family. Making memories and capturing others'. "I love it."

"I love you." He nipped at her earlobe.

"I love you more."

Locke chuckled. "I love you most. I did run into a twister for you."

Well played. "You win." She pecked his lips.

"I know." He traced her lower lip with his thumb. "I have you. And Lin." He kissed her nose, her lips, her cheeks. "I've won it all."

* * * * *

If you enjoyed this story,
pick up these other books
by Jessica R. Patch:

Cold Case Christmas
Dangerous Obsession
Secret Service Setup

Dear Reader,

Greer Montgomery was a tough character to write at first. Why would someone hide a child from a father if she knew he was a good man? It came down to her own childhood fears. Fear can be irrational, but it doesn't make it any less real or debilitating to the one who suffers from it.

Words hold life and death, and the words Greer heard her father say the night he left molded and shaped what she believed about men, especially men like Locklin, who had some similar playful and adventurous traits as Greer's dad. Greer had to learn to trust God. To trust that even if everyone walked out on her and baby Lin, God never would. When that peace was enough, it healed her to trust Locke and give him a chance to be the dad he desperately wanted to be, but was also afraid of.

You and I don't have to be afraid of our pasts or how they were shaped. We do have to be brave and ask God to heal us from those fears and help us trust people in our lives who want to help and love us. I hope you enjoyed Greer and Locke's story. I love to hear from readers, so please email me at jessica@jessicarpatch.com and sign up for my newsletter to keep in touch and be "Patched In" with all things bookish! Sign up at www.jessicarpatch.com.

Warmly,
Jessica

THE FORTUNES OF TEXAS COLLECTION!

18 FREE BOOKS in all!

Treat yourself to the rich legacy of the Fortune and Mendoza clans in this remarkable 50-book collection. This collection is packed with cowboys, tycoons and Texas-sized romances!